I0602129

FULL TERM

Full Term by Ellie Rose McKee

www.ellierosemckee.com

Copyright © 2021 Ellie Rose McKee

Second Printing - 2023

All rights reserved. This book or any portion thereof may not be reproduced or used in any manner whatsoever without the express written permission of the publisher except for the use of brief quotations in a book review.

Cover Photo by Samuel Borges

Paperback ISBN: 978-1-8384323-0-0

FULL TERM

Elowen Press

WWW.ELOWENPRESS.COM

The Family Ties Trilogy

- Book One: Full Term
- Book Two: Life Lessons
- Book Three: Drop Out

Author Note

Trigger warnings are listed on the back page of this book, to be read in advance—or ignored—at the reader's discretion.

Chapter One

The pain was getting worse. Mya gripped the edge of her desk, the tops of her fingers turning white. Her nausea had passed, and she'd been just trying to get through her last class of the day, but it had slowly dawned on her... that ship had sailed.

Out of the harbour, way out to sea, gone.

Earlier that morning, she'd been convinced that what she was experiencing weren't real contractions. She'd double-checked her guidebook, and it had said that fake contractions not only were a thing, but actually pretty common. At that point, the pains weren't that bad, and pretty far apart—a few times, she'd actually thought they'd gone away completely, only to pick up again—but now, there was no escape.

From the knowledge.

From the pain.

Hope had turned to denial, then a sinking kind of acceptance, and now, absolute, all-out panic. This hadn't been the plan. The due date she'd calculated wasn't for another two weeks. She'd had a plan! Why did the universe hate her?

Mya took a deep breath and raised her hand, her arm shaking. "Mr Daniels?"

He looked up from his desk. "Yes, Mya, what is it?"

"Can I be excused?"

Mr Daniels sighed and looked at his watch. "There's half an hour left, you can wait."

"No," said Mya, trying to keep her voice even, but the pain was cresting again. "I'm sorry, I can't."

"Might I remind you," said Mr Daniels, "the equations you're working on form a key part of your exams?"

"Yes, I know, but–" How could she think of equations, when she'd been trying to time her contractions, and even that was beyond her? Because she couldn't exactly sit staring at the clock—someone would definitely notice, sooner or later—so she just kept sneaking glances, except the pain made everything feel like it was taking forever, so when she looked back up, she could never quite trust what she saw. Like, had the second hand really only gone around once? No, it had to be twice. Except it didn't look like the minute hand had moved at all.

Her brain was playing tricks. But of course, her teacher didn't know any of that.

"Honestly!" he snapped, making Mya flinch. Mr Daniels always hated 'back talk,' as he called it. "You've had more bathroom breaks this past term than my incontinent poodle."

The class laughed and Mr Daniels glared at them. They studiously turned their eyes back to their workbooks.

"Please," said Mya, hating that she had to beg. "I'm really sick."

Mr Daniels sighed again. "Fine. But take Stacy with you, if you're all that bad."

The girl beside Mya looked up again from her desk. "Sir?"

Mya tried to protest, but Mr Daniels was having none of it.

"Go on!" he snapped. "You've already disrupted enough of my class."

They got up, gathering their books. Stacy grumbled under her breath that it wasn't fair he'd picked her, while Mya took extra care to make sure her jumper didn't ride up and accidentally expose her belly. She wore it baggy, but even so, it'd gotten really hard to hide her bump from certain angles.

More pain hit Mya the second she was in the hallway and she had to hurry her steps towards the girls' bathroom, pushing past a couple of guys in the way. She didn't pause to see who they were, and yelped when a hand landed on her shoulder, fighting her instinct to lash out at whichever one of them had put it there.

"Mya, are you okay?" Crap. That was Richard's voice. Her ex-boyfriend and father of her swiftly incoming child. This couldn't be happening. What were the chances she'd run into him here? And why had he picked now of all times to start talking to her again?

"Mya?" he repeated, his face full of concern that had her equal parts furious and gooey inside. Mya didn't feel well placed to deal with either. She could have deflected the question, asking how he and Ryan—his partner in crime who was stoically standing beside him—had gotten out of their own class, but even that felt too much.

"I can't," she said. "I have to–" She continued on towards the bathroom without finishing. She couldn't think, much less explain herself.

"Mya!" she heard Richard call after. "What's going on?" She thought that part might have been directed at Stacy, but didn't hang around to find out.

In the bathroom, Mya propped herself up against one of the walls and tried to work her way through some breathing exercises she'd seen in a YouTube video, but she couldn't remember any of the timings. It was like the pain had taken over her brain and she couldn't focus on anything else. She didn't know how much time had passed when she looked up and saw Stacy standing across from her, shifting from foot to foot.

"Are you okay?"

"What do you think?"

Stacy bit her lip. "What's wrong?"

A strangled laugh escaped Mya's throat. What was wrong? What was *right*?

"Are you and Richard getting back together?" Stacy asked, but Mya didn't answer. It wasn't anyone's business but theirs. And no matter that the answer was right there staring Mya in the face—that there was absolutely no coming back from what she'd done. From what she *was* doing, actively— she still couldn't bring herself to admit it out loud.

The truth stabbed her in the chest and she gasped.

"Listen," said Stacy, "I can–"

Whatever she was about to say was cut off by a rush of liquid: blood and amniotic fluid sloshing down Mya's legs and splashing her socks.

Stacy swore. Her eyes were wide and her mouth was hanging open.

Mya turned away, utterly mortified and not sure how to feel when she heard the sound of Stacy exiting the bathroom again a second or two later. Relieved to have been left alone? Scared?

Both. Definitely both.

Mya caught sight of herself in the mirror and gasped again, barely recognising the person staring back at her. Her normally honeyed-brown complexion had lost its pregnancy glow and now she was pale with fear and washed-out exhaustion. It made Mr Daniels not believing that she was sick completely ridiculous, but explained why Richard had suddenly gotten past his problem with her and looked like he had been about to slip into the caretaker mode he was always in around his mum and sisters.

She began to cry, silent at first, then gasping sobs that made her whole body shake. How could she have let this happen? Why had she pinned all her hopes on having got her due date right? Yes, the guidebook said most first pregnancies went full term, but that wasn't a guarantee. And at this point, she was doubting if she'd even calculated the dates right in the first bloody place.

All Mya did know for sure was that now she was not only having her baby practically in public, far from the care of the women's shelter she'd picked out, two towns away, but people had seen her in distress. Her classmates might not know what was going on with her, but that wouldn't stop them churning theories into the rumour mill anyway.

She spared a thought for what news Richard might get, and how he'd hear it. From whom. Yes, she should have told him herself, but she'd finally been ready, and then suddenly he hadn't been around or willing to listen.

Mya screwed her eyes shut, knowing she'd have to move past it. It was done, and the much more real danger had started flashing in her head, eclipsing the Richard one:

Someone was going to call her mum.

Mya just knew it. For all her plans and timings, she'd totally screwed up, and someone was going to call her home, ask for her mother, and then give the news to her step-dad instead.

She clenched her fist and thumped it hard against the wall, hating how powerless she felt. Hating everything. This was the worst possible outcome. Everything she'd feared since she found out. Her heart hammered and rushing water sounded in her ears. This was it. She was gonna get swept away.

Fuck!

The sobs in Mya's chest built again, then the pain of another contraction built again, pushing her sadness and fear aside, and when it reached a crescendo and she was on the other side, she knew what she had to do.

Mya pulled her phone out of her blazer pocket and typed 999, her sweaty finger poised to press the dial button when the bathroom door opened again and Ms Jenkins—a science teacher from the classroom next door—came in, her face going pale the second her eyes landed on Mya.

Mya thought her teacher might throw up at the puddle still expanding around her in all directions, but Ms Jenkins swallowed, rolled up her sleeves, and took Mya by the arm.

"It's okay. It's all right. We'll get you sorted." She didn't look or sound remotely sure, but Mya wasn't in a position to argue. Ms Jenkins nodded at the phone still clutched in her hand. "Did you call for help?"

Mya shook her head. "Not yet."

"Okay," said Ms Jenkins. "Come on, I'll take you to hospital in my car. You can call ahead on the way."

"Okay," agreed Mya, tears tracking down her cheeks as she let her teacher lead her out of the bathroom past the individual stalls. Richard and Ryan were gone from the hallway, thank god, though Stacy was standing outside. She smiled at Mya a little unsurely, and Mya nodded at her, grateful she'd gotten help.

She had that in her favour, if nothing else.

Chapter Two

The car ride to hospital happened in a blur. Mya got the feeling Ms Jenkins wanted to say something—probably ask her what the hell she was doing—but even though she kept opening her mouth, no words materialised.

By the time Mya was helped out of the car and into a wheelchair by a porter and rushed down a hallway, she had lost track of her teacher completely and assumed she'd gone home or back to school. Duty done.

Mya couldn't help but feel the sting of abandonment, but she knew it was a projection that had less to do with her teacher and everything to do with the people who really should have been there with her not actually being there. Which, given that she hadn't actually told any of them that she was pregnant, she knew she logically couldn't blame them for.

Logic didn't carry much weight with Mya's emotions right then.

A nurse appeared at her shoulder and asked her to confirm her name, address, and date of birth. Mya did so through clenched teeth, trying hard not to cry again.

"Who's your next of kin?"

The question hit her like a gut punch, and it was a moment before she could answer. What came first to mind was the list of people she *couldn't* rely on.

"M-my sister. Half-sister. Zhara." Mya called out the number she'd memorised when she was nine, and the nurse left her to make the call.

A midwife who introduced herself as Doris came in and got Mya stripped and into a hospital gown.

"Do you have to tell my parents?" Mya asked her.

Doris paused, part-way through putting on a pair of gloves. "Do you not want us to tell them?"

"No," said Mya. "Please don't. *Please.*" She was distantly aware that she was begging again, but had lost her ability to care about it.

Doris frowned for a moment, as if weighing options, then resumed putting on her gloves. "We don't have to call them right now."

Mya breathed a sigh of relief. Okay. It was okay. She had a stay of execution. Maybe it would all work out and–

"You're sixteen, right?" said Doris.

"Yeah," said Mya.

"How much prenatal care have you had?"

"Uh…"

The furrow between Doris' eyebrows deepened. "None at all?"

Mya worried her lip. "I, um, watched some videos. A-and read a book." Only hearing herself say it now did she realise how ridiculous it was.

"Well," said Doris, rolling with it, "obviously not ideal, but it shouldn't matter. Your main issue is that you won't be used to the intimacy of the examinations you'll need.

Most prospective mothers by this point will have already had a dozen hands inside them."

Mya shuddered and Doris forced a smile.

"You'll be fine. I'll talk you through what's going on. Here–" She produced a needle attached to a bit of plastic tubing. "This is an IV, to connect you to a drip." She nodded at a metal pole thing, with a bag. "It'll keep your fluids up."

"Okay," said Mya, still trying to take it all in. Because no matter how many videos she'd watched or how many times she went over the labour portion of her guidebook to 'pregnancy and beyond,' it just didn't compare to the real thing.

And boy, did it feel really freaking real now.

Mya was given an oxygen mask and blood pressure cuff. There was another needle that was apparently for a blood sample. Then the worst part, where a nurse came in—different from the one who had taken her details. They just flipped Mya's gown up and started wiping down her groin and belly, not taking the time or care to tell Mya in advance what they were doing, like Doris had. Mya considered ripping the nurse's head off, but Doris wasn't long in shooing them off. By the way she was glaring at them, it seemed like they'd be getting in trouble for their brusqueness, when all was said and done.

Mya took a little satisfaction in that.

"I need you to brace yourself," said Doris, hunkering down to be eye-level with Mya's crotch. "That means mentally. Come on now, don't tense up. It'll make it hurt more."

"Okay," repeated Mya. What she was being told registered as sense in her brain, but her brain was having trouble making the theory connect to anything practical. She understood that she had to be mentally prepared, but not bracing herself physically.

She hadn't the slightest idea how to do either.

"I'm just going to check your cervix," said Doris. "Okay?"

"O-okay." *Fuck.* Her voice was trembling. Mya had the feeling that Doris would be the type to stop what she was doing and make sure Mya was totally comfortable before continuing, in ideal circumstances, but these weren't those. Doris needed to get a move on and Mya just had to deal with it.

"First, I'm putting something into your urethra to drain your bladder," said Doris, not showing Mya what the 'something' was, for which she was glad.

The nurse who had taken her details stepped back in the room while the insertion was happening. She passed Mya her clipboard with some sheets of paper on it. "You'll need to sign these."

Mya's eyes were watering, but she did her best to focus all of her attention on the nurse and not what Doris' fingers were doing. Mya didn't think she could have read the words in front of her right then even with the best vision in the world.

"It's consent to cut you, if we need to. To help get the baby out," explained the nurse.

Some kind of noise escaped Mya's throat—even she wasn't sure if it was meant to be consent—but she reached for the pen and made her best attempt at a squiggle next to where the nurse had indicated with her finger.

Holy crap! It felt like Doris' whole hand was inside Mya. Which, she realised after the initial shock wore off, it probably was. She'd initially thought checking her cervix just meant looking, but belatedly realised that of course it involved feeling, too.

Doris had not been kidding about the intimacy thing.

"Looks like you're fully dilated," she announced. "Baby's definitely on the way."

"Great," said the nurse, taking the pen and clipboard away again, though Mya wasn't sure if she meant the signature or was responding to the dilation news. Mya expected her to leave, but instead she stood a moment longer, as if bracing herself. It was then Mya realised she had bad news and likely wasn't yet used to giving it.

"What?" she asked, the question coming out harsher than she intended. She was vaguely aware of Doris rising from her crouch and moving over to the side of the room. Did she look worried, or was it just Mya's imagination?

"We haven't been able to contact your sister," said the nurse.

Ugh! Another gut punch. "Have you tried?"

"Of course."

Of course. Mya knew it was a stupid question, but she hadn't been able to come up with a better one. She wasn't exactly at the top of her game.

"I'll keep trying," said the nurse, and she left again.

Mya returned her attention to Doris, who was having hushed words with someone Mya hadn't even noticed enter the room. He was an Asian man in a white lab coat. A doctor, she assumed.

She watched him and Doris talk a moment longer, not able to pick up on what they were saying, then everything kind of whited out in the strongest contraction she'd had yet. At some point, her body had started pushing all of its own accord. Mya had gone past crying and was struggling not to scream.

When the contraction passed, she watched in slow motion as the doctor approached her and introduced himself, a grim look on his face.

"Hi Mya, my name is Mr Lee. I'm a consultant here. You're in a bit of a pickle."

She stared at him, her eyes feeling like saucers in her head. "I am?" God, what was wrong? Was she having twins? Triplets?

"Your baby is in a tricky position," said Mr Lee. "They've got their arm above their head. It's called shoulder dystocia."

"Okay," Mya said again, suddenly sick of the word. She thought she'd read about the shoulder thing before, in her book. The section about complications. "W-what–?" She winced as another contraction ripped through her, then started panting. "What does–?"

"I need to put my hands inside you and see if I can get the arm moved," said Mr Lee.

And as horrifying as those words were, Mya didn't hesitate. She needed the baby out of her and she needed it now.

"Do it. Please, do it."

Mr Lee nodded once and got to work. It was the strangest sensation. Pulling and pushing and movement and pain. So much pain!

"Mya, I need you to stop pushing for a minute, okay?"

"I–I'm not–" She didn't know how to stop. It had come on like an instinct.

"It's okay," said Doris, taking her hand. "Focus on me. Deep breaths, okay? Deep and slow. Now hold it a minute. Yes, that's it."

The weird movements in Mya's abdomen continued, then there was a tug, and more movement.

Mya screamed and squeezed Doris' hand.

Doris rubbed the back of Mya's hand with the gloved fingers of her free one. "You're doing great. Hold still. Come on, now, relax. Just hang on, baby." Mya wasn't sure if she was talking to her or the actual baby at this point, but it didn't matter. It was all nonsense. How were either of them supposed to relax? It was stupid!

Time swam again, the pressure-y, sloshy movements continued, and then the first nurse reappeared. "I'm sorry, we still haven't been able to reach your sister. But your step-dad is in the waiting room. Shall I bring him in?"

Mya went cold.

A litany of swear words streamed through her brain, but she couldn't say anything out loud. The nurse repeated the question and Mya turned to Doris, willing her to understand and step in. Do something. *Anything!*

"Mya," said Doris, "are you okay?"

She shook her head. Mr Lee still had his hands inside her, pushing and pulling at her baby, and Kian was outside, and it was all too much.

"Are you safe?" pressed Doris.

Fresh tears leaked from the corners of Mya's eyes and she shook her head again. "No. He–he's dangerous. Please. I can't–"

"Okay," said Doris, "it's okay." She shared a look with the nurse, who went off again to–

"What's she gonna do? What's happening?" God, she could barely breathe.

"If your step-dad poses a threat, we'll have him removed."

"No!" It came out in a startled yelp that made Doris lean back for a moment, though she couldn't get far, with her hand still in Mya's deathgrip.

"You don't want him to go?" she questioned. "But you said–"

"He'll get mad," said Mya. If they made him leave, he'd go home and her mum would be for it. And she wouldn't know it was coming. He'd be furious and she wouldn't have enough forewarning to hide. Mya wondered briefly how he'd even found out, then figured the school must have called the house.

"Just focus on the baby for now," said Doris. "Everything else can wait."

That sounded like it made sense, but of course it wasn't that easy. Mya tried to argue, but she didn't have the strength. Or the words. Or anything. Whatever Mr Lee was doing—pushing the baby back in, by the feel of it, then twisting, turning, and trying to pull it back out—was making her feel ill. Was it supposed to take so long? Was the baby okay?

Almost as if reading her mind, Mr Lee spoke for the first time in—what had it been? Minutes? Hours? "I've gotten the baby's arm in the right place," he said, "but the cord is wrapped around the neck."

No. *No!* They were gonna die. Kian wouldn't even need to bother.

"I can unwrap the cord," continued Mr Lee, "but you'll need to bear with me a little while longer, can you do that?"

She couldn't. Mya couldn't handle any of what was happening. She and her baby were both going to die, and Richard would never even get to see his kid.

Despite the breakup, it had been part of Mya's grand plan to contact him when they were safe in the women's shelter and she could finally explain everything to him whether he wanted to hear it or not. She had to believe that once he knew the truth, he'd want to be in his kid's life. Even if he never forgave her for not telling him before now, she thought she knew him well enough to trust that he'd love their child just as soon as he saw it.

God, why did he have to be so pig-headed and stop her from telling him before? She'd gotten past her initial shock and found some courage, but he'd picked that moment to declare he was done listening, and done with her in general. If only he'd been a little more patient, he could have been with her now, but of course not. That'd be too simple. And now it was all too late, and everything was a mess, and goddammit, none of it mattered, because she was going to die!

"Please," she begged Doris, "call my–" Her brain stumbled on what to call him. "My Richard. Please, he needs to–I–"

"Where's the number?" asked Doris, not making her try and find the rest of the words. Mya pointed at her pile of clothes and Doris dug her phone out of her blazer pocket.

"His number is under the name Stacy. Tell him–"

"I'm on it," said Doris, stepping outside the room as once more, Mr Lee reached back inside Mya and tried to save her baby's life.

Ellie Rose McKee

Chapter Three

It had to be a nightmare. Some kind of anxiety dream. Because what other explanation could there be? How was it possible for things to just keep getting worse?

"There's a second loop," said Mr Lee. "Just a moment more."

It felt like an eternity, but eventually he said he'd got it. And then Mya was allowed to push again. That part, when it finally came, didn't actually seem that long. Not compared to the rest.

In the end, the baby slid from Mya like a fish.

She braced herself, expecting the sound of screaming, but nothing came.

Mya craned her neck and caught the barest sight of blue-ish, sticky skin.

Mya's vision went fuzzy, even as her brain turned on some kind of high alert setting. She was taking in everything, but could process nothing. More people swept into the room, seemingly from nowhere—Mya didn't know if they were doctors, nurses, midwives, or what—and no one was telling her. Everyone's attention had diverted to the baby, but that was fine by her. She knew just then, with absolute certainty, that she'd give anything for her baby. For it to live, and survive, and be okay.

Even if it meant she wasn't around to see it.

The new people were putting some kind of suction thing down the baby's throat. It still didn't scream, or cry, or make any noise at all. Was it moving, or was she imagining that?

Before Mya could overthink it too much, the mysterious hospital staff swept back out of the room, taking the baby with them. Mya felt bereft in their wake. What was happening? Where were they taking her baby, and would she ever get to see it? Her arms ached with how empty they were.

Doris was still outside, on the phone, or whatever, but a different midwife was trying to tell Mya something. She had to close her eyes and clench her jaw shut to try and focus on the words.

"They're getting the baby breathing," she said. "It's a girl."

Mya's eyes snapped open. A girl. She'd had a girl. A daughter. She–

Doris stepped back in the room. "Richard's coming," she said, setting Mya's phone back down on her pile of clothes.

Mya blinked at her, watching as she looked around. She saw the moment Doris noticed that Mr Lee had gone from in front of Mya, and Mya could tell she knew exactly what must have happened.

"Give me a minute," she said, and disappeared through the same door the team had used, not into the main hall, but to somewhere else. A resus room? A nursery?

In her absence, the second midwife stationed herself in front of Mya. "Doris will see you right," she assured her. "Find out exactly what's happening, and bring you the good news. In the meantime, we've got to deliver your placenta."

Mya felt her head nod automatically. *Doris will bring good news,* she repeated to herself. *It'll be good news. She'll be okay. My daughter. She—holy crap, I have a daughter! I'm a mum!*

"Come on now," said the second midwife, "keep your breaths steady. You can do it." She counted slowly, getting Mya to breathe in time with her words. When she could just about think again, Mya asked her name.

"Adela," said the midwife, smiling.

"Pretty," said Mya. She tried to smile back, but another contraction hit and she felt her face twist into a grimace instead. God, when was this going to end? What would happen if she simply couldn't find the strength to keep pushing? Screaming had weirdly helped, before, but now even that seemed like too much energy.

Just as Mya thought she might pass out from exhaustion, Doris came back into the room with a big grin on her face, and Mya found herself sitting up on high alert once more.

"Baby's fine," said Doris. "We have a heartbeat and steady breaths."

"Can I see her?"

"Oh, sweetie, no," said Doris, her smile dimming. "Not yet. Baby's in an incubator, and I can see you're not quite done here." She took back over from Adela and coached Mya the rest of the way through delivering the placenta. Thankfully, it was nothing compared to the main event.

"Now?" asked Mya, the second she had enough breath in her lungs again. "I can see her now?"

"Soon," Doris assured her. "Just after we get you stitched up."

"Stitches?" repeated Mya, a little dizzily.

"There was some tearing," said Doris, "but not much. You'll be right as rain in no time."

"Right," said Mya. It was just one thing after another. Again, she felt lost in terms of how long everything was taking, barely knowing if it had been minutes or days and already feeling some of the details from earlier fading from her memory. But the main thing was that her baby had survived. That, she knew for sure. Mya would be tempted to say that nothing else at all mattered, but then the original nurse who'd gotten Mya checked in came back into the room, and suddenly there was Richard, behind her.

Mya and Richard locked eyes and they both froze. In a single moment, it was like there was everything and nothing between them. Everything that had gone before: their first time meeting, in primary school, getting places in the same high school together, the first time he'd asked her out, and their first kiss. All their firsts, and now, a daughter. It was the whole world. Those six years and a tiny, wriggling child.

It should have been the happiest day of their lives. Except, when Mya looked at Richard, she could see a kind of emptiness had entered his eyes. Worse even than the day he'd broken up with her, because at least then he'd clearly been feeling something—even if they were not-good feelings. Now it was like all of it was gone, or maybe blocked, and instead there was a chasm. A wall. Mya could barely see beyond the betrayal and utter bewilderment on his face to the person she knew best in the world.

And it was then that the inevitability that had been building—circling, gathering speed— finally hit home, and Mya knew she'd broken them.

***

Richard looked away first. Mya thought he was in danger of turning around and walking right back out the door, except Adela ushered him the rest of the way into the room and produced a chair from the hall.

"Sit down and take Mya's hand," she said. "Your girlfriend's been very brave but she'll need you as we stitch her up."

Mya winced at the word 'girlfriend,' but it didn't seem the right moment to correct her midwife, and she could understand the assumption.

It seemed like he was acting on autopilot, but to his credit, Richard followed the instruction. His hand felt cold in Mya's, and she stared at it, scared to look at his face and take in all of his horror again. Mya's brain scrambled for something to say. Some words that might begin to explain herself, but then she felt the first prick of the needle and pain was all she could focus on until it was done. It was almost worse than all the contractions. Not quite, but almost.

Doris cast a furtive glance between Mya and Richard then asked him if he'd been told the baby was okay. Richard stammered a response and Mya shook her head at Doris, silently willing her not to ask anything else.

"I'll just go check on her," she said, taking Adela with her in a not-so-subtle attempt to give Mya and Richard some privacy to talk. "There's a button you can press if you need us."

Silence was heavy in Doris and Adela's wake. Mya thought about how she definitely needed help, but was pretty sure that the kind she needed couldn't be attained at the press of a button.

There were ten seconds where it felt like the whole world was on pause, then Richard—slowly, and not ungently––let go of Mya's hand and stood. Mya watched him pace the room three times before he looked up at her again, eyes glistening.

"So, you had a kid." His voice was broken, like the words stabbed his throat on the way out, and Mya felt the full weight of accusation in them.

"A girl," she said, still scared to talk but knowing that the time for hiding was well behind them both.

"Who is–?" Richard began to say, then cut himself off with the shake of his head. "I mean, I'm not, am I? It's not–She's–?" He gestured in the general direction the midwives had gone in and Mya felt fresh tears slip down her cheeks.

"She's yours," she managed to get out, though she wasn't sure how. It really hadn't occurred to her that Richard might doubt he was the dad, but of course he would, given the secrecy. Just another stupid thing at the end of a very stupid list. "Of course she's yours. *Ours.*"

Richard did not look relieved. He shook his head again. Rubbed at his temples. Resumed pacing, but slower.

"I–I know it's a lot to take in," said Mya.

He stopped and looked at her. A penetrating gaze that was so unlike her boyfriend it scared her.

"I know I can only imagine what it's like," she quickly amended. "What you're going through… but–" Shit, she was sobbing again. Great gasping breaths made her whole body shudder and all Mya wanted to do was scream at herself, because this was her moment. Her one chance to finally tell Richard everything and she couldn't speak with the weight of it pushing down on her chest. She couldn't see through all the tears, but after a minute, she felt Richard's hand return to hers. It was only a small thing, but it meant so much. That he cared. That, for the moment, he was still there, and wanting to help. Mya used the touch—the nearness of him—to ground herself, and when the majority of her grief passed, she looked again at Richard, sat there just as broken and lost beside her.

"Did you know?" he asked, then scrunched up his brow like he'd realised it was a stupid question. "You must have. When, then?" he asked instead.

"When?" repeated Mya. Of all the questions, that was the one he wanted to know?

"Yeah. When did you find out?"

"I…" It dawned on her a moment too late that what he was really asking was how long she'd been lying to him. For a while, she told herself it wasn't really a lie. It wasn't like she ever told him she *wasn't* pregnant, but of course she knew that didn't matter. Technicalities were meaningless.

"How long, Mya?" Richard pressed, his eyes hardening.

She swallowed but forced herself not to look away. "November. A couple of months after we… when we'd started…"

Mya hadn't thought it possible, but Richard's face fell more. "All this time?" he said, quiet now, like he was asking himself as much as her.

"I tried," said Mya. "You–"

"You didn't trust me." He said it like it was a fact, and everything within Mya rebelled.

"No!" she said. "No, you can't think that!"

He dropped her hand again, and it felt different, like he was throwing it away. "I don't know what to think! How am I supposed to handle any of this?"

"If you'll just listen," said Mya. "I can–"

"Explain?" he said. "Go on then."

But their time was up. Mya had no doubt Doris had given her as long as she could, but it wasn't enough. She came back into the room with the look of an apology, like she knew what she was interrupting but had no choice. Also like she'd heard everything.

"Mr Lee will be back with you in a minute," said Adela. "You'll have a chance to finally meet baby."

Mya's heart leapt. She could see her daughter, who was okay, and it would be fine. If Richard just looked at her, too, Mya was sure he'd see he was the dad and that–

"Wait! Where are you going?"

"Don't you want to wait for the doctor?" asked Adela. "He really won't be long at all."

"I can't," said Richard. "I can't do any of this."

And he just walked out.

Ellie Rose McKee

Chapter Four

Mya was torn in two. Richard had gone, taking half of her with him, and she was powerless to sew herself back up. But then––*then*––she was gently eased into a wheelchair and taken into another room, and there she was. Her baby. The little spark of joy that made everything else right in the world. Mya's hand reached out towards the incubator of its own accord, like the baby had some kind of magnetic force.

"She's so small," she heard herself say, distantly.

"That's not what you were saying an hour ago, when you were trying to get her out," joked Doris.

Mya smiled and glanced up at her, but just for a moment. She couldn't bear to look away from the incubator for longer.

"She's okay? Really okay?" Mya questioned.

"She'll be fine," said Doris, "just as soon as she gets a good feed in her. You planning to breastfeed?"

Mya felt heat rise in her cheeks. "That was the plan. Though I don't, um… I mean, what if I get it wrong?"

She hoped Doris would tell her there was no wrong way to breastfeed a baby, but what she said instead was, "We'll use a bottle if she doesn't latch, or if it hurts too much."

"Oh." *Breastfeeding hurts?* "Okay." She could kick herself for not reading the second half of her guidebook, on what to do after the baby was actually born, but Mya had been so sure she had more time. For so long, she hadn't really been able to see beyond the labour part. And now where was she?

"Can I hold her?"

"'Course," said Doris, opening the incubator and untangling the baby from tubes and wires.

"Does she not need all that anymore?" asked Mya.

Doris pointed to each tube in turn. "Measures blood pressure, heart rate, temperature. A lot of the same things you were hooked up to, back there." She nodded in the general direction of the delivery room Mya had used, that was now being prepared for someone else about to become a parent.

"And the mask? That's for oxygen, right? How can I feed her if–?"

"Told you she was breathing okay now, didn't I?" said Doris, cutting Mya off before her questions spiralled too far into all-out terror. "We were just giving her a little boost in the meantime. Come on now, slip your gown down, that's it." She lifted the baby up and unwrapped her from her blanket, setting her on Mya's chest so their skin was touching.

It was… weird. The baby's skin was so soft, and delicate, and had a really unusual smell. Not unpleasant—not at all, it was amazing, actually—but not like anything Mya had ever smelled before. Mya was surprised at how light her skin was. She'd expected her to be darker than her, because of how dark Richard was, but maybe her skin tone would change as she grew up. Mya decided it didn't matter, because she was beautiful. She was just sitting there, shifting ever so slightly, not doing anything else, and yet it was the most profound thing

Mya had ever experienced. Tears blurred her eyes and she felt foolish for it. It was on the tip of her tongue to say she was sorry, but Doris saw it coming.

"None of that, now," she said. "Perfectly normal. I'm always worried when new mothers *don't* cry at this part. Not that it happens often, mind."

Mya briefly wondered if her mum had cried over her, then shoved the thought swiftly aside.

"Do you want to give feeding a try?" asked Doris.

"Yeah," said Mya, nodding and sniffling. "In a minute. I just want to bask a bit more."

Doris beamed. "Take as long as you need. I've got to go check on another little one, but I'll be back in a tick."

Ridiculous as it might have been, Mya panicked at the thought of being left alone with her baby. She turned a little, towards the door, ready to tell Doris to stay, but this must have been commonplace, too, because Doris had paused, as if knowing this was the next step in a well-rehearsed play.

"You'll be fine," she said. "Already a natural."

Mya felt a smile touch her lips. "I don't know about that."

"Trust me," said Doris, "I can tell."

She was right about the being-fine part, at least, because she left just as she said she would and the world didn't end. By the time Doris came back, Mya barely registered the interruption. Having her baby right there, rising and falling on her chest, was the most calming thing in the world.

"Do I have to move her?" Mya asked in a whisper.

"Only a little," said Doris. "If you get a good latch, suckling will feel just as natural. There now." She got her resettled in the right position for feeding.

Mya waited a moment, expecting… she wasn't quite sure what. The baby was attached to her all right, but nothing seemed to be happening. "Am I doing it right?"

"Grand so far," said Doris. "It can sometimes take a minute or two for anything to come."

"Thank you," said Mya, looking up from her baby for only the third time since they'd been together. She caught Doris' gaze and held it, trying to infuse the look with all the sincerity she felt. "I'd be so lost without you."

"Och," said Doris, waving a hand, "what we're here for. Thank you for being a good patient."

Mya laughed. "Don't think I was one of those, with all the drama and all."

"Keeps the days interesting," said Doris, though for the first time, Mya got the sense it wasn't exactly what she'd been thinking. "Listen," she went on, changing tack, "you know what you said earlier…"

Oh, god, here it comes. Mya had so hoped she'd get longer to spend enjoying the relative peace of new motherhood, but of course things had to start catching up with her soon enough.

"There's someone who needs to speak with you," said Doris. She raised her eyes to the door and made a tiny 'come in' gesture with the nod of her head.

Mya blinked as quite possibly the tallest woman she'd ever seen stepped into the room and nodded to Doris in turn. She introduced herself as Tracy, the "nurse in charge of safeguarding concerns."

Doris went to leave again, and again Mya wanted to beg her to stay. She didn't this time, though. Just focused all of her attention on her baby as Tracy pulled up a chair and clasped her hands in her lap.

"She's beautiful," said Tracy, but Mya didn't answer. She knew it was rude, but she didn't fully care. Part of her felt betrayed, though she recognised that didn't make a whole lot of sense.

"Do you have a name?" asked Tracy, clearly desperate to get the conversation going one way or another.

Mya's resolve to not like the nurse didn't hold out very long. She watched her baby in silence for a minute, wondering if she should move her over to her other breast, since the little dribbles that were escaping didn't look all that much like milk as she knew it, from a carton.

All these months, Mya had been back and forth on what to call her child. Now, though, the choice was obvious. "She's called Emma," she told Tracy. It was the nickname Richard had for his grandmother, because he couldn't say Emmanuela growing up, though she didn't explain that part. "I'm thinking maybe Adela and Doris as middle names."

"Lovely," said the nurse, and before she could turn the conversation to what it was really about, Mya cut her off.

"She doesn't have to have his name, does she?" she asked, irrationally scared of the answer. Tracy looked puzzled and Mya clarified, "Emma. It says on her oversized plastic ankle tag thing 'Baby Byrne.' I guess 'cause that's my surname, but..." She bit her lip, not entirely sure how to explain. Looking down made it easier. Focusing all of her attention on Emma. On breathing in the new-baby scent of her.

"Byrne is your dad's name, is it?" asked Tracy.

"Step-dad," said Mya. It was a very important distinction.

Tracy nodded, just at the edge of Mya's vision. "The man who was in the waiting room earlier."

"Yeah," she said, her voice quiet even to her own ears. It was hard to know what she was feeling now, beyond exhaustion. Besides Emma in her arms, who was everything.

"Mya, you made a very serious allegation to one of your midwives," said Tracy.

"I did."

Tracy paused, clearly waiting for Mya to elaborate, but she wasn't sure where to find the words. They'd been locked inside her so long, and then they'd slipped out, but she hadn't planned that. Everything was most definitely, one-hundred-and-two percent off-plan.

"You don't have to talk to me," said Tracy, and Mya almost felt relieved, but then she went on to say the fatal word: *but.*

"What you've said is called a disclosure. We have passed it on to social services, but they're going to need a little more before they're able to do anything."

"More like what?" asked Mya.

"Well," said Tracy, "as disclosures go, yours didn't have a lot of detail–" Mya looked back at her, ready to snap, but Tracy held up her hands. "I'm not criticising. For you to have said anything at all is an incredibly difficult thing to do, especially under the circumstances." She graced Emma with another soft smile. "What you said was brave, and that's good."

She said 'but' again and Mya winced. "What do you need?"

"Just enough detail to turn your disclosure into a full disclosure."

"Then what?"

"Then I speak to social services again, they talk to you, and turn your full disclosure into a formal statement."

Mya groaned, already hating it. She got that there were systems and procedures. They probably made a lot of sense to someone in an office, somewhere, but she just wanted to hold Emma forever. And maybe sleep at some point.

"Do we have to do this now?"

Tracy gave her a considered look, firm but not without sympathy. "If we're to keep your step-dad out of here, yes. I believe you told Doris you were worried about him leaving, too. Do you want to tell me about that?"

Mya sighed. "My mum. I didn't want him going home and taking it out on her."

"Have you got brothers and sisters at home?" asked Tracy. "Anyone else who could be in danger?"

"No. My sister—half-sister—lives somewhere else," said Mya. "She's over eighteen." It was the second time that day that Mya had qualified Zhara's status as her sister with the word 'half,' which was not normally something she allowed herself to even think about, much less release into the world.

It hurt too much. But she thought maybe it might matter to the hospital staff. They seemed a little focused on technicalities.

"Okay," said Tracy, moving the conversation on again. She probably didn't want to be having it any more than Mya did. "So, you're worried about yourself and your mum. Why is that?"

"M-my–" God, her voice was already shaking. She had to close her eyes and clear her throat. "My step-dad. Kian. He, um… he hits my mum."

"Has he ever hit you?"

It didn't matter how softly the question was asked, it hit Mya right in the ribs and she whimpered, hating how fragile it made her feel. "A few times," she admitted. "Not recently. My, uh… My mum. She tends to get in the way. Draw his fire."

"Okay," Tracy said again. And she stood up, making Mya open her eyes and look at her.

"That's it?"

"It's enough for now," said Tracy. "When social services talk to you, it'll be more in depth, but you've given me enough to pass on and get them out here."

"Oh. Well, um, thank you."

Tracy smiled again, this time at Mya specifically, rather than just at Emma. "No," she said, her tone sincere, "thank *you*. You've done something really big and important here."

Mya nodded, not sure how else to respond. She kind of wanted to cry again, but didn't want to do it in front of Emma. Not sad tears. If this was only the tip of the iceberg, which Mya was starting to believe it was, then there would be plenty of shared tears ahead of them. There was no need to get a head start on them now. *No, let's have her first day be totally sad-tear-free.*

"I'll leave you to it," said Tracy, slipping from the room. Mya watched her go down the hall through the still open door. With every step Tracy took, Mya felt her heart thud, and as she looked back down at Emma for what easily had to be the thousandth time at this point, she wondered if either of them could be ready for the can of worms Mya had just opened in their lives.

Chapter Five

The day after Mya talked to the safeguarding nurse, a social worker showed up, as promised. She was a white woman called Jane, middle-aged, and seemed nice enough. Jane took a formal statement from Mya and discussed 'next steps.'

"There will be something called a MARAC meeting," she said. "It stands for Multi-Agency Risk Assessment Conference."

Mya thought it sounded awful. "Do I need to be there?"

"No," said Jane. "There will be representatives from the police, social services, the health service, and probably the domestic abuse service, too. Yours will only be one of the cases we'll be discussing."

"Right." It felt kind of surreal. Like some kind of reality TV show about a courtroom, except less exciting. Certainly a world apart from double science after lunch. "So, this meeting... Everyone there will talk about me, and make a decision?" she questioned. "About where I go?"

"Yes," said Jane. "I'm going to refer you for counselling, and recommend the housing team find you a place in a Mother and Baby Unit."

"Is that like another ward of the hospital?" The word unit had a definite 'institution' vibe to it. But Jane surprised Mya by saying no.

"It's a completely separate building, broken up into several blocks. Other side of town and nothing to do with the hospital. If we can get you in, you'll have your own room but will have to share communal spaces with a few other mothers. You'll have someone called a keyworker who lives on site, who you can go to for help, but for the most part you'll be independent. How does that sound?"

Mya wasn't sure. It very much felt like adulthood was rushing up to slam her in the face, and she wasn't sure she was ready—except, she reminded herself, she was a parent already. Ready or not, this was her life now.

"Better than going home," she said at last, sparing just the briefest thought for all the things she'd left behind, likely to never see again. She'd have to buy everything from a toothbrush to clothes, and maybe a hairdryer. Though where she'd get the money, she had no idea yet.

Jane looked ready to pack away her folder and go back to her office. Mya watched the calm efficiency of her, wondering what she really made of a sixteen-year-old single mother with nowhere to go. As soon as she thought it, her brain caught on the word 'single' and she flinched, which spurred her on to ask about Richard.

"Have you spoken to him?"

"Him and his parents both," affirmed Jane.

"And?" Mya pressed.

Jane pursed her lips and paused a moment, as if making a decision. "You want the truth?"

No, thought Mya, terrified. But she couldn't not know. "Tell me."

Jane set her folder back on the table of Mya's hospital bed. She was in a regular maternity ward now, with Emma in a crib beside her. "Richard's very upset," said Jane. "It's been a big shock. His parents are eager to meet Emma, but Richard doesn't feel ready."

"And I bet none of them want to see me," said Mya, which Jane didn't confirm or deny, something she took as a confirmation in itself. Man, it stung. The only way Mya could bear it was to press on with the next order of business. "Have you spoken to my mum?"

"Well," said Jane, "no. A specialised police officer went out to the house and invited her to make a statement, but she declined."

Mya could have sworn. It didn't matter that she'd expected it, it was another slam to the face. Forcing maturity into her voice that she didn't quite feel, she acknowledged that it must have been a big shock to her, too. And then she had to look away from Jane, because she knew that part was her fault, for not saying anything.

"I'm not going to lie to you, Mya," said Jane, "the police won't be chasing your mother for a statement. As far as their resources go, they need to focus them on people who are willing to work with them. I know it's a disappointment, and hard to hear, but without your mum's statement, their hands are tied."

What? No. That couldn't be right. Mya told herself she must be misunderstanding something. "*I* gave you a statement. Can't they use that to arrest Kian? I'm sure my mum will talk when he's not breathing down her neck."

"The officer who spoke to your mother will have followed protocol," said Jane. "She would have made sure your mum was alone when she talked to her."

Mya shook her head, knowing all too well that it wouldn't have mattered. Kian didn't have to be literally standing beside you to cast a shadow over everything.

"Unfortunately," Jane continued, "you're only a third-party witness to your mum's abuse. And we don't have any evidence of him hurting you. You told us yourself that he didn't hit you while you were pregnant."

That was true. Mya had been extra careful to stay out of his way and tried her hardest not to piss him off the whole time, in case something happened to the baby, but a lot of it was luck, too. "Why does that matter?" she asked, not able to make sense of it.

"For him to have endangered an unborn child would have been another strike against him," said Jane, "something you *could* have testified against."

Mya groaned, hating that Emma's relative safety so far was being used against her. Or at least that's what it felt like. She regretted not lying, but it was too late for that. Changing her statement now would only make it all worse.

Fuck. She balled her hands into fists, using the sharpness of her nails digging into her palms to ground herself. It was all she had to stop blowing up or running down the hall screaming. She could get out from under Kian's roof, but he'd still be walking around. Of course he'd find her, sooner or later. Which meant she and Emma were no safer now than they had been before, and it was all for nothing. The agony and monotony of disclosures and statements, being asked the same difficult questions over and over again. The torture of keeping quiet. The fresh hell of losing Richard. All useless.

"The police will have referred your mum's details to the domestic abuse service," said Jane, no doubt trying to make it a little better. "They'll follow up with her in a couple of days and carry out a welfare check on the house. Hopefully she'll be ready to talk then. If she is, they can get the police back involved."

Mya sighed, exhausted by the ups and downs of everything she'd said and been told. The small hope wasn't much to cap it all off with, but she'd take it. Jane lifted her folder again and said she'd be in touch with the decision from the conference.

***

Jane had indeed been able to secure a place for Mya in a Mother and Baby Unit. At first glance, it wasn't quite the haven she had expected.

Outside, the exposed brickwork looked old and was chipped in places, like someone had spent years kicking a football against it. Paint was peeling off the front door, and although the floors and interior walls looked clean enough, there was an atmosphere. Not unwelcoming, exactly, but kind of cold. Impersonal. There was a painting in the communal lounge/kitchen area, giving the room a bit of colour, but it was just a mass-produced print, like the ones Mya had seen for sale in Wilko for fifteen quid.

That morning, Mya and Emma had been discharged from hospital and Jane had picked them up, taking them right over to meet their new keyworker, Patsy, who was now explaining how everybody had their own cupboard and a designated shelf in the fridge.

Sharing the unit was Katie, who had a one-year-old. She kept her head down, avoiding everybody's eye, which reminded Mya of her mother. There was Lynne, who was very pregnant—she grunted a kind of greeting—and Bernice, whose kid looked maybe a couple of months. Bernice made such a show of being welcoming, it set Mya's teeth on edge. She stuck out like a sore thumb, being the youngest one there, and the only person of colour. Something Bernice was kind enough to mention.

"Oh, won't it be great to have some diversity around here!" she said to Lynne, who rolled her eyes but didn't otherwise reply.

Mya opened her mouth to tell her new flatmate that she was a person, not some statistic or token minority, but, "Yes, well, anyway," said Jane, swiftly moving the conversation on before Mya got any further. "Here you are." She gave Mya a card with her phone number on it, and a pack of emergency supplies that she said had been donated by a local charity. It had shampoo and soap, but no conditioner; three toilet rolls, a small hand towel and face cloth, but no bath towel; plus nappies that were about three sizes too big for Emma.

The lack of conditioner was gonna be a problem. Mya's post-hospital hair was already set to be a nightmare to detangle even with the help of product, and almost impossible without it. But it wasn't like she had the energy to think about showering right then anyway. The baby supplies issue took priority, and she could figure out the rest later.

Mya felt both ridiculously grateful and horribly embarrassed at the same time. She couldn't help the tears that came after Jane left and she sat alone on her small, stiff bed, just looking at the small pack sitting alongside her school bag. In the kitchen, there was a box with her name on it containing rice, long-life milk, and a small assortment of cans—baked beans and vegetable broth.

It was all Mya had in the world, aside from Emma. Mya thought she could bear anything, so long as she got to keep Emma with her, but it all seemed so impossible. She wasn't sure how she could care for herself, much less a newborn. The reality of independence had started to sink in as she realised she'd have to borrow plates and cutlery for a while. A can opener and bowl at the very least. Though what if her new flatmates didn't want to share? Mya couldn't really blame them if they didn't. They didn't know her, after all, and if they were living there, that meant they were probably in the same position. Imagine if someone new came in and asked Mya for bread or a cup of sugar or whatever. All she'd be able to do was stare at them, likely speechless. But there was water in the tap, and now that she'd started breastfeeding, Mya's boobs felt like a tap she couldn't turn off, so Emma wouldn't go hungry.

Just so long as Mya herself didn't starve to death.

As she contemplated that cheery thought, someone banged on her bedroom door, making her jump.

"Hello?" she said through the wall, furious that her voice shook a little.

"It's Lynne," came a Yorkshire accent from the other side. "You comin' for a fag?"

Mya paused to consider the offer. She didn't smoke, and didn't know what to make of the other woman at all, but, well, there was only one way to make something of her, and Mya didn't want to be alone—she had plenty of that to look forward to, later—so she wiped roughly at her eyes and stood up, stuffing her feet back in her shoes.

"Just a minute!"

By the time she'd wrapped Emma up in a blanket and made her way into the hall, it was empty. Mya looked around, wondering if Lynne had gone back into her own room, but made her way outside when all she was faced with was a line of closed doors.

There was Lynne, puffing away on a cigarette in a small, makeshift smoking area in a corner of the paved yard. She eyed Mya closely as she shuffled over and got Emma settled on her lap.

"So, what's your story then?"

Mya almost laughed at the directness of the question. After she'd hesitated for too long, Lynne said, "You're just right, bein' cagy. Can be tricky, getting close to folk."

"Right," said Mya, because she honestly didn't know how else to respond. "What's *your* story?" she asked Lynne in turn, figuring that if she was okay asking the question, she was probably fine answering it.

"Me?" Lynne questioned, taking a long drag on her cigarette. Her eyes turned a little glassy, as if she was remembering something far in the past, or looking way out into the distance. Seeing as there was a brick wall not five feet in front of them, blocking their view of everything, Mya had to figure it was the first one. The pause went on so long, she started to wonder if she'd done the wrong thing, turning the question back on itself and horribly offending her new flatmate in the process, but then Lynne just started talking, like she'd been just waiting to be asked.

"Was raped by my dad for years," she said, her tone entirely casual. "Bastard managed to get me pregnant when I was seventeen, and I was stupid enough to want to keep it, but baby didn't make it. Social services found out and put me in the system."

Lynne pulled out another cigarette and lit it using the end of her first one as she continued a summary of her life story. Openly and honestly—almost cavalierly—she told Mya that from there she ended up in a string of emotionally and physically abusive relationships and got pregnant again at twenty-two, leaving her last boyfriend when she found out.

"Been moved around temporary accommodation since, ending up 'ere last week. Baby won't be long now, they reckon."

Mya's eyes felt huge in her head. She swallowed and steadied her gaze on the back of Emma's hat-covered head, lest Lynne think she was judging her or whatever. "I thought I had it bad."

Lynne blew out a long stream of smoke, making Mya cough. "I used to think that, compared to what some others told me."

Mya looked up then, surprised, and Lynne laughed, deep and throaty.

"You thought I was the worst one?" She shook her head and took another drag. "Nah, mate. Not by a longshot. But you know what?"

"What?"

Lynne leaned in conspiratorially close and Mya resisted her impulse to recoil at the invasion of her personal space. "It don't matter. Not if it's the worst, or not that bad. Ain't some pissing contest. A person can drown in a puddle just as well as they can in t'ocean."

Huh. That was… Mya frowned, surprised again to recognise the wisdom of it.

Lynne grinned at her. "You can have that one for free. Now then, I'm bettin' you ain't got nowt to eat beyond that crappy little box they gave you. I'm havin' myself beans and toast for tea, so you're welcome to share until you get sorted."

"Oh," said Mya, feeling embarrassment flare in her cheeks again. "Thanks. I'm, uh, not actually sure how to get sorted."

"Not to worry," said Lynne. "There's a food bank down t'road. It's open tomorrow, and Patsy'll walk you through fillin' out forms to get you benefits, if you ain't already on them."

Mya shook her head, indicating she was not. She thanked Lynne again for the information, even while inwardly criticising Jane for having neglected it. Though maybe it was her own bad for not thinking to ask.

"Anything else you need to know, give us a buzz," Lynne finished, stubbing out her third cigarette in a row. "I'd steer clear of Bernice, if I were you," she added then.

"Yeah," said Mya, "she seems a little…"

"She's a bitch," said Lynne. "Was all cheery wi' me, on day one. Changed her tune when she didn't like how I hang up my undies, or chew my food. Went running to Patsy, making out I was trying to intimidate her or some bollocks."

Mya's had to snap her mouth shut to stop herself catching flies.

"I'm pretty sure she snoops, too," Lynne continued, "but don't take my word for. Jus' keep an eye out, yeah?"

"Uh, yeah," Mya mumbled, making a mental note to keep her door locked, even when she was inside.

Lynne stood up and stretched, then leaned down to stroke Emma's cheek. "Cute one you've got there. Girl, is it?"

Mya nodded.

"I'm sure she'll be a right handful," said Lynne, as she made her way back inside. Her tone of voice made it sound like it was something to look forward to.

Mya stared after her, even less certain of her new flatmate than she'd been before.

Back inside, Mya found Bernice standing in the middle of the corridor with her arms folded. She frowned, cast a backwards glance at the closed bedroom door behind her, then said in a stage-whisper, "If you want my advice, you'd be better off not associating with the likes of her."

"Her?" Mya questioned, because pretending like she didn't know who Bernice was talking about seemed like the safest bet.

"Lynne," said Bernice, "she's bad news."

Mya made a non-committal noise and stepped closer to her own door, trying to indicate that she didn't want to take part in any conversation slagging off someone else, but also not wanting to give her new flatmate any reason to think she was completely rude, in case she became the new object of criticism.

Bernice threw up her hands. "Well, on your own head be it," she said, and flounced off into the kitchen.

Mya sighed, much too tired for drama, even minor flatmate squabbles.

Despite the fact that she had clear issues, Mya found that she kind of liked Lynne. There was something about her that seemed genuine. While Bernice seemed the opposite, Mya had to remind herself that she didn't know either of them, yet, and Bernice had tried to welcome her, even if she was terrible at it. So, she'd give them both the benefit of the doubt and see how things played out. After all, Katie could be the true dark horse, masterminding the petty rivalry. Mya smiled at the absurdity of the theory, kind of glad that it was actually the worst thing she had to worry about, for the time being.

Chapter Six

It was pitch black when Mya was jolted awake, first by the sound of some kind of siren, then by Emma screaming in response. Disorientated, it took her a second to figure out where she was.

After a moment's fumbling, she found the light switch, ever grateful to discover that it worked, even if it did dazzle her vision.

Mya crossed the room to Emma's crib and picked her up, cuddling her to her aching chest. Mya's heart was beating so fast, she thought it might jump out her throat.

She pulled the curtain back to look outside, but couldn't discern anything particular through still sleep-filled eyes. Going out into the hall, she discovered the noise wasn't just in her room, but seemingly coming from all directions at once:

A fire alarm in every room and corridor.

Mya figured they must be all connected to the same system, and even though she couldn't smell smoke, it didn't mean some other part of the complex wasn't ablaze. So she hiked Emma higher in her arms and followed signs for the exit, glad they were marked, because she couldn't quite remember the layout of the place with her brain in panic mode.

When she was outside in the courtyard, she vaguely recalled having seen a notice up in the living room when she'd had dinner with Lynne, saying something about an assembly point. Had it been the yard itself, or out on the main road? She couldn't remember, but reasoned it was more likely to be across the street, so as to not be too close to falling things or whatever.

A stone caught in Mya's foot as she shuffled across the tarmac, waiting for cars to pass. She swallowed down a yell, not wanting to distress Emma further. There were no traffic lights for that part of the road, and she didn't have slippers. Only when she'd reached the relative safety of a car park facing the Mother and Baby Unit did Mya look back, and then it occurred to her that she was alone.

Why had no one else evacuated? Should she have gone down the hall, banging on doors to wake them up? She shook her head, telling herself that if the alarms didn't wake them, she'd stood no chance. But why hadn't it woken them? Surely, they couldn't have all been out for the night, or… she didn't actually know what time it was, just that the moon was still high in the sky.

Mya shivered and rocked Emma, who was still screaming, but not with quite so much force. It took a little while for the adrenaline that had slammed into Mya's system to dissipate, and then she could really feel the cold. She was just in pants and her oversized school jumper, after all, not having access to proper nightwear. A couple of people passed her in the street, giving her queer looks, and she grit her teeth, forcing herself not to react.

Her eyes were trained on her new home, looking for signs of smoke or flames—even a twitching curtain—but there was nothing. Mya shifted her weight from foot to foot, trying not to put too much pressure on her baby toe, which was now bleeding. Just as she wondered if either she had gone mad or it was the rest of the world that was insane, the alarms across the street stopped blaring, pretty much all at once.

Mya waited, wondering if it meant it was safe to go back inside. Maybe she had got the wrong assembly point after all, and everyone else was on the other side of the building, wondering where the hell she was. She could imagine Patsy ticking off names and then tapping her pencil beside Mya's name, annoyed she was MIA and holding up everyone else from going back inside. A dozen or more other scenarios flit through her head. That it was a drill, maybe, and no one else reacted because they'd expected it, but who ran fire drills while it was dark out, and why hadn't anyone told her?

She groaned, annoyed at herself for not having lifted her phone on the way out. But wasn't that what they'd been told in school: don't stop to take anything with you?

Just as it started to rain and Emma seemed ready to fall back asleep, Mya spotted someone coming out of the gate to the courtyard. It was kind of hard to pick out the details of their face, but she thought it might be Patsy. Only having met her once, alongside a string of other new people, Mya barely recognised her, in pyjamas and with dishevelled hair as she was. She waved to Mya, beckoning her to come, so she went, slowly back across the street.

"What are you doing out here?" It was indeed Patsy. "You'll catch your death of cold. Come on now."

She made her way back through the gate and courtyard, then down the hall into Mya's ground-floor flat, Mya following at her heels feeling like a scolded puppy. She wanted to say something about the assembly point, and not being sure where it was, but she felt stupid for her uncertainty. Everyone else seemed to know what was happening, after all.

Finally, Patsy turned and looked her up and down. "Jesus, don't you have a nightie?"

Mya bit her lip, fighting against the sudden urge to cry. Patsy seemed to pick up on her distress, because in a much more soothing voice she explained that the alarms going off was a regular occurrence.

"Can be up to three nights a week," she said. "People smoking in their rooms, or setting them off on purpose."

"Seriously?" exclaimed Mya, her feeling of foolishness giving way to irritation. Aside from bafflement as to why anyone would *purposefully* create all that noise, she wondered how she was expected to know if and when there was actually a real fire. She said as much to Patsy, who shrugged. "I mean, if everyone ignores the alarms, they might as well not be there," Mya continued, genuinely freaked at the thought of it.

"Listen," said Patsy, sounding tired, "you want to bring it up at the weekly meeting? Be my guest. In the meantime, I'm going back to bed."

Mya frowned but did the same, figuring she didn't have much choice. Only after she'd closed her door and turned around did her eye catch on her school bag, sitting open in the middle of her bed. Mya blinked at it, taking a moment to replay the whole stupid scenario over in her mind. Nope, there was no way she'd put the bag there. Which meant someone else had been in her room. Mya shuddered, but it had nothing to do with the cold now. Gingerly, she inspected the bag, pulling some things out with one hand as she still held Emma in the crook of her other arm, before going back into the hall and catching Patsy before she turned out her bedroom light.

She didn't look best pleased to see Mya up again. "Yes?" she said, trying and failing to keep frustration out of her voice.

Mya felt her own frustration rebound in response, but she did her best not to snap. "Someone's been in my room."

Patsy's eyes opened a little wider. "What makes you say that?"

"My bag was moved and–"

"Was anything taken?" asked Patsy, all business now.

"No," said Mya. "At least, not that I could tell. I–"

"Well then," said Patsy, visibly relaxing again, as if everything was suddenly resolved. "Make sure you keep your door locked."

Mya stared at her a moment, then, "Night," Patsy said pointedly and closed her door. Mya heard her lock it from the other side, taking her own advice.

"Well then," she repeated to herself, going back down the hall and closing herself in. Every cell of her body was on edge, but Mya focused her attention on getting Emma settled in her crib again, and damped some toilet roll to wipe the blood off her foot before climbing back into bed, not ready to turn the light off yet.

She just sat there, trying to come to terms with this new set of events. On their own, they might be minor, but all put together, it was more than Mya felt she could bear. Not on top of what she already had going on. She tried to sort her feelings into neatly labelled categories, but so many of them were stuck part way between one thing and another. Frustration and fear. Anger and tiredness and—ugh, what was even the point trying to sort stuff? It didn't change anything.

Folding herself into her scratchy duvet, Mya dug around between her bed and the wall until she found her phone, lodged halfway under the mattress. She didn't have much credit left, after trying a million times to call Zhara while she'd still been in hospital and just getting her voicemail, but Mya planned to soothe herself by looking through photos of her and Richard. She knew it'd be bittersweet, not least because none of them were recent, but even that didn't matter, because when Mya picked up the phone and pressed the button to light up the screen, what she saw blanked all of her thoughts and worries and plans from her mind.

Instinctively, she dropped it on the bed. Then, a couple of deep breaths later, when she told herself she was probably imagining it was worse than it was, or that she'd misread, she picked the handset up again, her fingers feeling numb.

There it was, in plain black text from an unknown number:

I'm gonna kill you and the brat both, slut.

***

Given Patsy's lack of concern for fire safety and the thought of someone going through her belongings without permission, Mya waited until the sun had been up for a while and she could hear her flatmates moving around the kitchen before she went to find her.

She hadn't gotten back to sleep, after the text.

Mya had just sat there, quietly seething, until Emma had needed fed. Then she'd kept her by her side long after she'd finished nursing and drifted off again. Mya kind of envied her ability to do that, no matter that everything was falling apart around her. To be so oblivious must be bliss, she thought—except not being aware of danger didn't protect you from it. If Mya was as clueless as Emma, they'd probably be in even more danger.

So, in a twisted way, the threat made some things easier. Concrete. Having no doubt in her mind that the text had come from Kian, seeing it settled some things in Mya's mind. Her resolve to be hypervigilant, for one thing, washing away all her uncertainty about how Kian was taking things.

Because yeah, of course she'd known he wouldn't be happily singing to himself and sending well wishes into the universe, but it was weirdly reassuring to know that he'd gone down the cold and calculated route rather than the other, blind drunk approach he had to things he didn't like. Mya had known she'd see or hear from him sooner or later, and had been waiting for it, which was a kind of torture in itself. Now, she was free from that. The threat was real, and immediate,

50

and not going away, but she didn't have to worry herself sick about when or how it would arrive.

Honestly, Mya wasn't sure if how she felt about it would make sense to anyone but herself, but she held onto the small scrap of sense anyway. And she didn't sleep, lest something else terrible creep up and blindside her.

Patsy called the police, when she told her, which was another relief.

Mya hadn't been sure what to do if her keyworker just shrugged it off—call Jane, probably, and fight off the urge to yell at them both. She was really starting to lose faith in the systems surrounding her and how much they wanted to keep her safe.

Jane arrived pretty much the same time as the cop car did, but stayed long after. Beyond taking a screenshot of the text and inspecting Mya's phone, there wasn't a great deal the police could do from the Mother and Baby Unit. A male officer said they'd try and track the source of the text, but he didn't seem real confident it'd get them anywhere. Apparently there were websites you could use that did a scarily good job of keeping your location hidden—something about VPNs—and, at first glance, that seemed to be what Kian had used.

Jane said the main thing was that it was logged, and made Mya promise to let them know if she got any more. "It's all evidence and it could all help in the long run, if the sender slips up and forgets to hide his identity," she said.

Mya tried not to think about how it all basically meant the grand plan was to sit around and wait until she was threatened again. Or worse.

"Do you know if the domestic abuse service has contacted my mum yet?" she asked Jane.

"They tried," said Jane. "A few times, from what I understand. They don't seem to be able to reach her."

Mya looked up from her tea, made using a borrowed tea bag with no milk or sugar, because she still didn't have any. "Can't reach her. What does that mean?"

Jane looked like she was picking her words very carefully. After a pause she said, "They called on the phone and there was no answer. Then someone went around to carry out an in-person welfare check, and your mum wasn't there."

Mya stared at her social worker, horrified. Her mum never left the house. Absolutely *never*. Which meant... what did it mean?

"My mum is missing?"

Chapter Seven

Mya had a full-on meltdown when Jane implied, but refused to outright say, that her mum was basically gone and no one had heard from her. Not that there was anyone who *could* have heard anything. It wasn't like she had friends, and she didn't really talk to Mya, even before Mya had actively distanced herself to keep her from accidentally finding out about the pregnancy.

When Mya had calmed down enough to hear what she was saying, Jane asked her permission to contact Zhara about where their mum might be. Mya had said there was no way she'd have gone to her sister, but she was more than welcome to try.

"Good luck getting her to answer her phone," she added bitterly.

Jane chose not to respond to that part. "I'd also like your permission for something else," she said, carrying on as if they were talking about dinner plans, or something.

Mya raised her eyebrows. "What now?"

"Well," said Jane, "I have to do this even without your say-so, because he has a legal responsibility, but it'll go better if you're on board. I want to try and make contact with your biological father."

Mya didn't say anything, and Jane gave her a minute to sit there, letting everything be absorbed by the silence. Then, gently, "Did you hear what I said?"

Mya nodded. She tried to speak a couple of times before any real words came out. She'd honestly never thought she'd see her dad again. And even the *possibility* that the long-held belief wasn't true shook her. "I need some time to think about it. Is that okay?"

"I can give you time, of course. You and Emma are the priority here. We want you to feel like your needs are being met. But don't leave it too long because, as I said–"

"Legal responsibility," Mya repeated, "yeah." The words made her feel numb. Her dad hadn't been responsible, maybe ever. It didn't fit to have him and responsibility in the same sentence. But if Jane needed to talk to him and would have to, sooner or later, it was just another thing Mya would have to come to terms with. Her gut instinct was to say no, and not give her blessing, but… well, she had a little while to find it.

•••

It took three days of no major incidents pulling her thoughts and feelings elsewhere, but Mya finally made up her mind and called Jane to say she was okay with her contacting her dad, if she could find him.

After that, it was time to sit down with Patsy to face all the benefit paperwork. Mya was surprised by how much there was. The way people on the news always talked about it, she'd assumed getting money out of the government was easy.

No such luck.

"You'll need to apply for Housing Benefit to cover rent," Patsy was explaining. "There used to be Unemployment Benefit and Child Tax Credit to help with living costs, but now it's all been rolled into Universal Credit. There's also a nursery funding component, if you want someone to mind Emma when you go back to school."

That one pulled Mya up short. Both the thought of leaving Emma with strangers, and going back to school. Was that something she wanted? She hadn't really thought about it.

"Let's leave that part for now."

"Fine," said Patsy, "but it takes weeks to get all these sorted. Sometimes months. Don't take too long making up your mind."

"I won't," Mya promised. "I'll think about it."

Patsy showed her where to sign on the other forms, then shuffled them together and slipped them into a folder.

"How much is it?" asked Mya.

"What you'll get?" questioned Patsy, and Mya nodded. "Different for everyone, but don't expect much. Government will throw you off them again, first chance they get. Keep your eyes peeled for other opportunities."

"Right," said Mya. She was fully convinced she wouldn't see any opportunities no matter how wide she opened her eyes—what was she going to do, walk past a shop with a sign in the window asking for a sixteen-year-old with a newborn?—but she didn't feel there was any point saying that.

"Good," Patsy said, packing up the rest of her things and heading for the door.

Mya watched her go, wondering what exactly Patsy's story was. Had she gone through such a home herself? Mya didn't think she was in her job just to help people, but who knew? Mya smiled to herself as she realised Lynne undoubtedly had more than a few theories. She made a mental note to ask her later and went back to her room for the time being.

Once there, Mya saw the notification light was blinking on her phone. She lifted it with shaking fingers, half hoping it was Richard saying he'd changed his mind and wanted to talk to her, and half terrified it was Kian sending more poisonous messages.

It took Mya three attempts to unlock her phone, but when she did, she saw it wasn't either of her imagined options, but a text from Zhara.

Did you have a baby? it read. That was it. Just one question.

Mya tried to call Zhara, but there was no answer, so she texted back: *Need to talk to you. Call me.*

A second later, the phone rang.

"Did you have a baby?" Zhara asked again, without preamble, when Mya picked up.

"Yes," said Mya, bracing herself.

There was silence for a second, then, "Shit, Mya, you had a baby!"

Mya laughed, because the response was very typical of Zhara, then had to fight off tears, because it was just so good to hear her voice. "Can I see you?" she asked, feeling like a little girl, begging for her big sister's attention.

"When?" asked Zhara.

"Uh…" Mya rubbed her eyes. "Now?"

Zhara thought about it for a moment, then said, "Yeah, okay. I can pick you up. Where you at?"

Mya gave her the address and then it wasn't long until they were sitting in the middle of the shopping centre food court, eating McDonalds. Mya had to shamefacedly admit she couldn't even afford the Happy Meal she wanted, and Zhara had dug around in her pockets for enough change to cover them both.

"Listen," said Mya, "I know this is awkward, but…"

"Spit it out," said Zhara, taking a sip of her Fanta.

"Well, have you got any more money?" asked Mya, making her sister's eyebrows go up. "I'm sorry," Mya continued. "I wouldn't ask, but it's just that I don't really have… well, anything." *Gah!* Her voice cracked and tears were threatening to overwhelm her again. *Stupid hormones.*

Zhara asked what she needed, specifically, and Mya listed off the most pressing items: a towel, and a toothbrush, conditioner, and something to wear to bed.

"All right," said Zhara, after another considered sip of her drink. "I can probably swing that. Your hair does look awful. But tell me what happened." She nodded her head at Emma, who was sleeping in the baby carrier Jane had got for her, somewhere.

Mya ignored the jibe, focusing instead on finding the best place to begin. She pulled apart three fries before saying, "I was scared to say anything. Because of Kian."

"I get that part," said Zhara. "But how come you had her at all? Who the hell you been sleeping with? And don't you know how to be careful?"

Mya felt heat rise in her cheeks. "God! Yes, okay? We were using condoms. I don't know what went wrong, but… And it wasn't a one night stand. I have a boyfriend. Or–" She face crumpled. "I had one, anyway. He, uh, didn't take the news so well."

Zhara narrowed her eyes. "I gotta beat him up?" she asked, all sincerity, and Mya barked a laugh.

"What? No!" She sighed. "He just needs time, I guess."

"Hmm," said Zhara, clearly reserving judgement until she got more details.

"Well, first I was in shock," Mya explained. "Then I was scared shitless for a bit. I wasn't worried Rich would be mad, just that he'd tell his folks."

"And then they'd call home," said Zhara, following the line of logic. "So, you just didn't say anything? You could have explained why. Asked him not to tell anyone else."

Mya rubbed her forehead. She'd already been over this so many times in her head, and she knew she'd screwed up, but she supposed she'd have to get used to admitting that out loud, too. "I was going to," she told Zhara. "The timing was never right. We were always in between classes or something. I wanted to do it right. But then Rich figured out I was hiding something, so he started getting weird about it."

"Weird how?" asked Zhara.

"Just weird," said Mya. "Annoyed, I guess. He kept asking me what was wrong, but that only made me clam up more, so he'd get frustrated. It was this stupid vicious circle. I finally found a time where we could be alone, without people around. I told him I wanted to talk, but he said he wanted to go first. I let him, like an idiot, not knowing he was gonna break up with me."

"*Shiiiit*," said Zhara, drawing the word out as she leaned back in her chair. "I bet he thought you were cheating. Or gonna dump him first."

"Yeah," said Mya, "maybe." She pushed her tray away, her appetite long gone. "I was so stunned, I didn't say anything after all. He walked away, and then things were awkward. He didn't want to meet me again. And, so…" She shifted in her seat, uncomfortable.

Zhara didn't say anything to that part, one way or another.

So "anyway," Mya continued after a minute, changing tack because she couldn't think any more about Rich right that second. "Let's talk about the more recent major development."

"Eh?"

"Um, Mum being missing?"

Zhara choked on her burger. "Back up, what?"

Mya tilted her head at her sister. "You didn't know? I figured you'd talked to Jane, which is how you knew about Emma."

"Who's Jane?" asked Zhara, making Mya even more confused.

"Uh, my social worker?"

"Oh." Zhara went back to her burger. "Her. Yeah, I had a message from someone. I guess it was her. She said she needed to talk to me, and I asked her why. Eventually, she told me about you, but I haven't gotten around to actually meeting her. Not sure I want to."

"Zhara, you have to meet her!" said Mya, horrified at the thought of her social worker just getting blown off. What if she gave up on Zhara the way the police gave up on their mum, and then Mya had even fewer people to lean on? She didn't think she could lose anyone else. Her support circle, as Jane called it, was already less of a circle and more of a dot. Yeah, she'd had friends in school, but as much as Mya hated to admit it, even to herself, she was one of those people who was all about her relationship. Her friends weren't so much hers as her and Richard's both, and she hadn't been too popular with any of them since the breakup. None of them had even messaged after she left school in active labour.

"I don't have to do anything," said Zhara, leaning back in her chair again. "So, what's the deal with Akosua?" She pointedly didn't call her 'mum,' though Mya was glad she'd used her name rather than any of the swear words she often called her instead.

"That's the thing," she said, "I don't know. Someone went to talk to her, and she wasn't home."

Zhara stopped rocking in her hair and sat up straight. "She was gone?"

Mya nodded.

"But she's never gone," said Zhara.

"I know," said Mya.

Zhara frowned. "You heard from Kian?"

Mya hesitated, not sure whether to tell her about the threat or not.

"I'll take that as a yes," said Zhara.

"Listen," said Mya, not wanting to get too far off the topic of Akosua. "What my social worker wants to ask you about is if you know where she might be."

"How would I know?"

Mya groaned, frustrated. "Just, if you had any ideas that'd be helpful," she said. "I'd really appreciate it if you'd at least talk to Jane."

Zhara set her jaw. "And what if I don't care if Akosua's found?"

"I know you do," said Mya, but Zhara didn't reply. She took out her phone and started scrolling, as if she didn't care about anyone or anything at all, but Mya knew it was a front. If she admitted she cared for their mum, she'd have to be scared.

"Listen," Mya said again, not willing to give up, "you know Mum's not–"

"She's not my mum," Zhara snapped.

"Bullshit," said Mya, utterly sick of how many times they'd had this conversation. Zhara needed to get past it and it had to be now. "I don't care what a DNA test would say. She raised us, so she's our mum."

"She lied to us," Zhara shot back. "To me. And let that monster into our lives. You think you'd be in the shit you're in now if she hadn't?" She'd raised her voice, and people were staring, but Mya couldn't back down.

"Letting him in wasn't the problem. You know he can sweet-talk people. She couldn't have known he was like that." No, the problem had been letting him stay after she found out.

"Whatever," said Zhara.

"What if he's hurt her?" Mya pressed, lowering her voice to counteract Zhara's shouting. "More than usual, I mean. What if she's–?" She couldn't finish the sentence, but they both knew how it ended.

Zhara sighed. "I don't know anything, Mya."

"I know," she said. "I know, just…" She clenched and unclenched her hands, not sure what else to say or do.

"I'll talk to your precious Jane if she calls again, yeah?" Zhara said finally.

Mya sagged in relief. It probably wouldn't change anything, but at least it wasn't a roadblock. "Thank you," she said, but Zhara waved it away.

"You done?" she asked, taking the trays before giving Mya a chance to answer.

They walked out into the carpark and were about to get back into Zhara's beat-up Corsa when Mya paused and looked back at the shopping centre. Seemingly reading her mind, Zhara said, "Got no funds 'til Friday. I'll get you sorted with stuff from my place."

Mya breathed a sigh of relief, grateful she hadn't forgotten, and that she didn't need to beg for charity a second time to remind her. "Thanks."

They drove to the other side of town, Mya watching rain trickle down the windows as they went. She'd never actually been to Zhara's place before, and wasn't sure what to expect.

Zhara pulled up outside a block of flats that had half of its windows boarded up. Mya had resolved to say something positive about the place, regardless of what it looked like, but as she took in the weeds coming up through concrete that someone had spray-painted with slurs, all she could manage was, "Which one is you?"

Zhara pointed to a window that wasn't boarded up and Mya looked up to see a woman looking back at her. Young, with blonde hair.

"Who's that?"

"No one," said Zhara, turning off the engine and taking the keys with her. "Wait here."

Mya watched her go, trying not to feel too disheartened about not being invited in. A part of her had actually hoped Zhara would let her stay, to get her out of the Mother and Baby Unit. She really didn't know what kind of life her sister lived, these days, but she had a pretty good idea that Zhara wanted to keep it that way.

Thankfully, Zhara wasn't long in coming back to the car, plastic bag in hand. She started up the Corsa again and set off, taking Mya home.

It was weird, thinking of it as home. Hell, everything was weird. It had been a week since Emma was born, and the whole world was upside down.

Chapter Eight

It didn't matter that Emma was far too young to play with anything, or even know what was happening right in front of her face; Mya took her to the local Mums and Tots group because she needed to get out of the flat before she strangled someone—Bernice or herself, she didn't know which.

All morning, Bernice had been driving Mya and Lynne mad. Probably Katie too, if she ever said anything to indicate what she was thinking. Bernie—as they called her just because she hated it—had drawn up a cleaning schedule and stuck it to all available surfaces, following up by taking great pains to explain each bullet point. As if there could be any confusion about instructions such as 'wipe down the surfaces after cooking,' or 'use a coaster!'

"Thinks she's the queen of the world, she does," said Lynne, when Bernice disappeared into her room for more Blu Tack.

Mya had sighed and shook her head, surprised to see Katie had cracked a grin. She looked away, embarrassed, when Mya smiled back.

Her little girl, Sarah, more than made up for her mother's lack of speech by babbling away happily to herself and anyone else who'd listen. Mya asked Katie, under the guise of posing the question to Sarah, if she wanted to go to Mums and Tots, but Katie responded by bundling Sarah up and going to hide in their room.

Mya turned to Lynne with eyebrows raised, mouth half open in preparation to ask her what her deal was, but then Bernice came back with Post-It notes and Sellotape and Mya decided she could wait to find out and made her break for it. She'd already asked Lynne if she wanted to go with her, but she'd said she had a doctor's appointment.

So Mya set off on her own, not entirely sure why she felt nervous but very aware of her clammy palms and heart running double time. By the time she got to the church and looked in through the big windows to see a crowd of women in their twenties and thirties who were all chatting like they'd known each other for years, Mya almost turned back. Bernice was annoying, but she wasn't an actively bad person, as far as Mya could tell. At the very least, she was a known quantity compared to the people inside.

Torn, Mya hovered near the door until she felt someone step up behind her. Her heart leapt and she turned sharply, relieved to see it was just another mum—one closer to her own age, at that.

"First time?" she asked, and Mya nodded. The woman held out her hand. "I'm Becky."

"Uh, hi." Mya rubbed her hand on the jogging bottoms Zhara had thought to include in her carrier bag of borrowed items and gave Becky the quickest handshake known to man. "I'm Mya. This is Emma."

Becky beamed. "Hi Emma!" She turned to the little boy who had half hidden himself behind her legs. "Miles, don't you want to say hi to Emma?"

Miles shook his head and Becky laughed. "Always takes him a little while to get warmed up. You going in?"

Mya bit her lip, feeling every bit of Miles' anxiety, but told herself she didn't have the excuse of being a three-year-old. "After you," she said, and followed Becky's lead.

It didn't turn out to be half bad, once she'd broken the ice with that first person. Becky introduced Mya to a string of people she could never hope to remember the names of, plus Steve, the group's token stay-at-home dad. *Or, wait. Was it Simon? Whatever.*

There was singing and free play and, most importantly, complimentary tea and biscuits. Mya took a custard cream and two digestives and was eyeing up a pink wafer when Becky came up beside her again. "Go for it," she whispered. "They're not rationed."

Mya turned away from the pink wafer.

Becky shook her head, but she was still smiling. Mya wasn't sure if she'd ever seen any person smile so much. Almost as soon as she thought it, though, Becky's smile dimmed as her face turned thoughtful.

"Tell me to butt out and mind my own business, but can I ask you a question?"

Mya eyed her a little suspiciously. "What's the question?"

"Well, you're young, aren't you?" said Becky.

Mya urged the floor to open and swallow her up. As she waited, no response came to her.

"I'm sorry," said Becky. "That was quite possibly the worst way for me to word that. I'm only asking because I was fifteen when I had Mister." She gestured to Miles, who was sharing his biscuit with a rag doll in the corner of the room. "I know what it can be like."

"Oh," said Mya, relieved she wasn't going to be treated to some judgemental remarks or insensitive questions. "I'm sixteen."

"Same age as my sister," said Becky. "Don't suppose you know her? Goes to the Academy on the hill."

"What's her name?" asked Mya, warming to the conversation, now it wasn't directly about her.

"Stacy," said Becky.

Mya frowned. "Stacy Limpet?"

Becky's face brightened. "You *do* know her!"

"Yeah," said Mya. "She's in my class. Or was in my class. What, uh, used to be my class." Suddenly feeling exhausted, she gave in and reached for the pink wafer to sustain herself. "Listen, it was really nice to meet you, but I should really go home."

"Sure. It was nice to meet you, too. Miles, come and say goodbye."

Miles didn't even look up from the heated discussion with his doll.

Outside, Mya took three deep breaths and told herself it was fine that she was shaky. It wasn't just the new faces, or the new place, or the questions, or even the reminder where she would be if she hadn't a tiny human depending on her for everything. It was all of it, combined.

She thought about Stacy as she walked back to the Mother and Baby Unit. About how they'd never really gotten along, but how Stacy had gotten help the moment she realised Mya was in labour. Had she been thinking of her sister at the time? Maybe having a flashback? As if Mya hadn't already been painfully aware, it reinforced the fact that you really didn't know what went on in the background of people's lives.

Meeting Becky and seeing how obviously happy she was gave Mya a small glimmer of hope for how things could turn out for her. When she reached the courtyard outside the flat, she sat in the smoking area, not quite ready to go back in.

She wanted to bask in the glimmer, just a bit, and not run the risk of having Bernice steamroll right through it.

Between the hope and the weird sense of loneliness that a room full of strangers could give you, Mya instinctively took out her phone. She'd been trying so hard to give Richard the space he needed, but one call couldn't hurt, right?

She pulled up his number, feeling weird about the fact that it was still saved under Stacy's name. A series of short clicks, and she changed it. Two more, and it was ringing. Mya held her breath, nervous he wasn't going to pick up, but he did. Almost immediately, as if he'd been waiting for the call. Mya thought it was a sign—fate, or something—but then he spoke.

"I can't talk," he said. "I'm sorry." And he hung up.

Mya stared at the phone. Her vision started to blur, and her hand started to shake, and then she heard the sound of the gate opening to the courtyard and rubbed quickly at her eyes with the back of her hand, the phone shoved quickly back in her pocket.

"Ay-up, duck. What's wrong?"

Mya didn't answer and Lynne didn't press her, even as she came over and took the seat opposite.

"You want a fag?"

Mya took one wordlessly, mostly so both her mouth and hands would be occupied, but she couldn't get the lighter to work.

"Here," said Lynne, passing Mya her already lit one and taking the new one back for herself.

Mya stared at it for a second, then took a drag, just like she'd seen thousands of times on TV, even if she wasn't sure she was holding it right. She only inhaled once, but it was enough to make her eyes water again and throat close up. She coughed until she thought she thought she might throw up, and Lynne thumped her back, which hurt but also weirdly helped.

When she no longer feared for her life, Mya went to throw the stupid thing away—except she didn't. Pausing, she considered the cigarette afresh. And then she put it back to her lips. It wasn't so bad the second time, the burn of the smoke in the back of her throat not quite as harsh.

That's not good enough. With everything that had happened and was still happening, Mya wanted to be in control of her own destruction for just one minute. She kept inhaling and coughing, planning to go back for more until either she really did throw up or ultimately feel better, but Lynne snatched the cigarette from her hand before it was even halfway gone.

"Oi!" she said, "Take it easy, won't you?" She carefully tapped it on the wall, putting it out but not crushing it, then slid it back in the packet. "Those ain't cheap."

"Sorry," said Mya, feeling foolish on top of hurt and stupid and embarrassed.

Lynne waved a hand. "So, what's got you lookin' like a slapped backside?"

Mya felt the corners of her mouth turn up in a smile, despite herself. She fiddled with the little toggle on her coat. "Can I ask you a question?"

"Aye."

Mya frowned, trying hard to figure out how best to word what she wanted to know. "Your, um…" She looked up at Lynne again, who was studying her face carefully. Mya cleared her throat. "What you said before. About your past boyfriends…"

"Ah," said Lynne, knowingly. "Man trouble."

Mya felt heat rise in her cheeks but chose not to confirm the remark. "So, I was wondering…" She trailed off again.

"Go on then," said Lynne, "I gotta go inside in a minute. This one's got me at the loo every ten bloody minutes." She rubbed her belly with a fond look on her face, which somehow gave Mya the confidence to spit her question out.

"You said about your past relationships. About them being bad. Were they all like that?"

Lynne looked into the middle distance for a long moment, her cigarette frozen halfway to her mouth. "There was one bloke. Good sort."

Mya sat up a little straighter. "Yeah?"

"Yeah," said Lynne, using a soft voice that Mya didn't recognise. She paused again, sniffed, and then shook her head, resuming smoking.

"What, um–? I mean, did he–?"

"I broke up with him," said Lynne. "Got back with this one's dad. Was a right bastard, he was."

Mya tried to process that. She didn't want to pry any more, but what Lynne had said didn't compute. After everything, she'd found a great guy and then gone back to someone terrible?

"I don't get it."

Lynne shrugged. "Hard to explain. Wasn't exactly thinkin' straight."

"Fair enough," said Mya. It wasn't, really, but what else could she say?

Lynne nudged her arm and she raised her eyes from where they'd drifted back to the toggle on her coat. "Listen," she said. "Your bloke. He the good sort?"

"Yeah," said Mya slowly. "I think he is."

"Good," said Lynne. "Don't give up on him. Even the good ones mess up, and can find it hard when we've hurt them."

Mya blinked at her, wondering if she knew more than she was telling. But how could she have known about Richard and their stupid fight?

"Take it from me, duck," said Lynne, standing up. "Give up on 'im and you'll regret it."

Mya went in behind her, going directly to her room where she could cry in private. She thought about what Lynne had said—about Richard, but also about regrets more generally.

About her mum.

She knew she had to do something to try and find her, but still didn't know where to start. All she knew for sure was that if she needed help and Mya hadn't done everything she could, it would be a much bigger regret than calling her boyfriend when she shouldn't.

I have to assume she's not dead. Because—well, I have to. So that means she's somewhere. If it's not at the house, and she's obviously not with me or Zhara, then what? Some kind of shelter, maybe? Mya shook her head, dismissing the idea. If Akosua was in a shelter, Jane should have heard about it, and she'd have said something.

Mya kept coming back to the idea of family, but her mum didn't have any. At least not that she ever spoke of. Obviously, she'd had parents at some point, but Mya always assumed they were still in Ghana. *What if that assumption's wrong, though?* She resolved to do a little digging, but was distracted by her phone beeping. Hoping it was Richard texting to say he was sorry for being so abrupt, or saying anything so long as he'd speak to her, Mya took the phone put of her pocket and looked down at it.

A text, but not from Richard.

Another threat, but vaguer than before: *You're gonna regret ruining people's lives, bitch.*

Mya blinked, not sure if she was seeing things, because it didn't make sense. The sender hadn't been masked, and it wasn't Kian.

Chapter Nine

"Let me get this straight," said PC Grant. This time, it was a youngish black woman who took Mya's statement while someone else inspected her phone. "The new text you received was from someone already in your contacts."

"Yes," said Mya, using her last bit of patience not to put a sigh at the end. They'd been over things three times already, and the PC still didn't seem to be getting it.

"Your phone says the text is from someone called Denise. Who's that?"

Mya rubbed her forehead. "Denise is just some girl from my school. But she didn't actually send it. That's not her number. I've barely spoken to her and have never had her number."

PC Grant scrunched up her nose, like she was concentrating. "So," she began again, but Mya cut her off.

"Look," she finally snapped, "my step-dad abused me. Amongst other things, he was really controlling. He'd check my phone and demand to know who everyone was. If I'd had a guy's number stored, the interrogation would have been worse. So, any guys I knew, I just put them in beside someone else's name. Like an alias or whatever. Do you understand now? Do you?"

Mya stopped, breathless, all the words swirling around her head. No matter that she'd already made a disclosure and a formal statement about Kian, she hadn't ever actually used the words 'my step-dad abused me' before. Not all in a row like that. She'd been scared to, but now that it was out, Mya felt light. Almost like she could float away. And she wondered why she'd ever been so terrified. It seemed so simple, now she'd done it.

When she turned her attention back to PC Grant, Mya saw something had changed in the way she was looking back at her. "Okay," she said, drawing a line in her little notebook under what she'd already written. "So, who's the mystery sender?"

Mya frowned, because this was the part she couldn't get her head around. "It's Ryan."

PC Grant wrote down the name and looked up again, expectantly.

"He's my boyfriend's best friend. Well, best friend besides me. Except–" She cringed, because she kept falling into that same trap. "My boyfriend isn't exactly my boyfriend right now. We, uh…"

"That shouldn't matter," said PC Grant, "unless it bears on the case. Do you think it does?"

"I…" Mya wet her lips. "I'm not sure. I guess that's what it's about. What Ryan said—he had to be talking about Richard."

PC Grant glanced up from her notes and Mya clarified, "My boyfriend. Uh, *ex*-boyfriend." God, this was a mess.

The PC nodded, as if she'd heard Mya's thought. "I think that'll do for now. We'll speak to Ryan and get back to you. Do you know his address?"

Mya didn't, exactly, but she told PC Grant his surname and the estate he lived in. When she and the officer inspecting her phone left, Jane—who had been standing silently off to the side—walked across the kitchen, over the little line that divided it from the living area, and sat down at the dining table beside Mya.

"Well," she said, "it might not feel like it, but this is progress."

"I guess," said Mya, though she wasn't sure she actually agreed. She'd been so sure the first text had been from Kian. And if it wasn't, then it was like she'd lost evidence against him, and was even less likely to get him put behind bars. So, if anything, discovering it was Ryan harassing her felt like a huge backwards step.

But she couldn't dwell on that. She knew she couldn't, or she'd never be able to dig her way back out of the wallowing. Mya turned her mind to other matters, and was on the verge of asking Jane if she'd be able to look up records for her mum—a family tree, or something—when Jane said, "I want you to brace yourself."

Every muscle in Mya's body tensed as she imagined what words were coming next. Had they found a body? Would she need to identify it? What if–?

"Mya, are you okay?" Jane was looking seriously worried.

"Just tell me," said Mya, holding her breath.

"I've found your father."

***

Mya had spent extra long getting ready the next morning—putting her hair up, taking it down again, attempting to smooth out the lines under her eyes with her fingers—but eventually it had been time to go.

Jane had come around again to pick Mya up, as she was meeting her dad at Jane's office, in a special room which Mya assumed was designed for just such an occasion as long-lost parents walking back into their children's lives.

There were throw pillows in varying shades of blue dotted across two sofas, which faced each other, with a white coffee table in the middle that had plastic things on its corners to stop people banging into them, damaging themselves or the table.

Jane was minding Emma during the proceedings, and someone else had put out water in a plastic pitcher, two matching plastic tumblers, and a selection of biscuits on a paper plate. But no matter how well prepared the room was, or how much Mya had fussed over her hair, she didn't feel ready. She had no idea what she'd say, despite having thought of nothing else all night.

Or for the past eleven years.

She'd paced the room three times when someone appeared on the other side of the door, obscured by a panel of frosted glass. Mya braced herself, but then the handle turned, the person stepped in, and she exhaled, returning to her task of wearing a hole in the carpet.

"Wrong room," she told the person—a white guy who looked old as dirt, and not actually that white, considering how pronounced his jaundice was. Mya recognised the symptom of yellowed skin from her baby book, but she hadn't actually known adults could get it until right then. Not that it mattered. It didn't affect her. She just needed whoever he was to buzz off and find an unoccupied space so that she could–

"Mya?"

She stopped short. Stopped pacing. Stopped thinking. Almost stopped breathing. And then turned, slowly, to look again.

"Mya?" repeated the man. His voice had a shake in it. And, she noticed, her gaze sweeping the length of him, his hand had a shake, too. "Is that you?"

Mya couldn't answer. It was like she was in a fairy tale, and someone had stolen her voice. She shuddered, fighting the instinct to cry, because she may not have recognised her dad, but she certainly knew the voice, shake and all, and the realization ripped through her like a jagged knife. Only Richard leaving her alone in the labour ward had hurt more.

Silently, the man came the rest of the way into the room, shut the door, and sat down, the heavy musk of old smoke following him. The man who had walked out on her and Zhara, leaving a massive, miserable hole that Kian came along and filled with hatred and fear. Their father. David Wilson.

Mya sat down opposite him, because it was either that or fall over.

"You're here," she heard herself say, though the words sounded alien.

"So are you," said David. He tried to smile, but ended up in a coughing fit that took him scarily long to recover from. So long that Mya asked if he needed her to go get someone— call Jane down from her office upstairs, or call an ambulance. David shook his head and Mya poured him some water instead, but he didn't reach for it.

"What's wrong?" she asked, when he'd finally stopped coughing, but he shook his head again.

"Aren't we here to talk about you?"

Is that what we're here for? Jane had said she had to contact him, for some legal reason, but it wasn't like they could just start catching up now. Fix everything, and move on. There were a million questions lying unasked on the coffee table between them, but Mya wasn't sure they'd do any good. There was no answer to, 'why did you leave?' that would ever make it okay.

"You look good," said David.

"No, I don't," said Mya. "I have, like, two sets of clothes, and one of them is my school uniform. I'm overweight, and also not eating enough, since you can only get certain things from the food bank. I'm always exhausted, and have giant bags under my eyes. Don't you come in here with pleasantries and lie to me and waste my time."

David pursed his lips and his gaze changed, like he was assessing her as an enemy he had to fight, or win over. Exactly like someone at the benefit office he had to convince to give him the bare minimum to live on, actually—something Mya now sadly had first-hand experience of.

Mya resented the look and all it represented. She'd been anxious, but she hadn't known just how angry she was with the man in front of her until he was actually in front of her. It was all the anger Zhara had for their mum, except freshly dug up.

"What do you want me to say?" David asked at last, and Mya felt a strike of inspiration. Because maybe he might be useful, after all.

"Does Mum have any family? Here, in England, I mean?"

David's eyes turned cold, part hurt, part disappointed. But what did he expect? It wasn't like he'd even been the one to finally get in touch. Jane had set up the meeting, otherwise he would still be absent, living whatever life he had without his daughters, far away from them both.

No, Mya didn't feel sympathy. Even if he did look like death. If anything, it made her more angry, because he could have died and they wouldn't even have known.

"I need to know," she pressed.

David sighed. "I don't think her parents ever left Africa."

Mya's resentment buried that little bit deeper. It drove her nuts when people spoke of Africa like it was a single place, and not a huge continent made of lots of countries.

"They're probably dead now," David added casually. "Though I suppose there's always Mouse."

Mya blinked, relayed the sentence over in her head, and then looked at her father for some kind of clarification.

He laughed, and then started coughing again, finally reaching for the water.

"Mouse?" Mya questioned, because there was no way she was just going to let the topic lie there, and David clearly hadn't picked up on her interest organically.

"Mouse," he repeated. "You know, your aunt."

Mya just stared.

"You don't know about your aunt?" He shrugged. "I suppose she always was a bit of a shrew, pun not intended. Never liked me. Always thought your mother was lowering herself."

I can't imagine why, Mya thought but didn't say, even while another part of her brain was stuck on the new information. Why had she literally never heard of this woman? Who was she? And, more importantly, *where* was she?

"Is that actually her name? Mouse?" Mya was dubious, but if she could confirm a name, it might just be the lead she needed.

David scoffed. "She had some African name. Mouse is just what I called her."

Mya clenched her fists but did her best to keep her face unreadable. She hoped it worked. "Do you know anything else?"

"Mya," said David. "Can't we change the topic?"

No, she wanted to scream, but held her tongue right at the last moment. "Sure, what do you want to talk about?"

He visibly floundered for a moment, then asked, "How's school?"

Mya rolled her eyes. She couldn't help it. "Did Jane tell you anything about me?"

"Well," said David, "she said you might need me."

Mya would put money on her social worker definitely not having said that. At least not in that way. "Did she say why? Did you even ask?"

"Mya," said David, sitting forward suddenly, "why do I feel like I'm on trial here?"

She raised her eyebrows. "You really have to ask?"

His gaze fell to his shoes, but he didn't lean away again. "You could go easy on an old man."

"I could," she allowed. "I don't really want to, but…" Mya sighed. "Do you actually want to get to know me? Is that why you're here? What about Zhara? And–"

He looked up again, panic in his eyes. "I wanted to see how you are," he said, "that's all."

Mya's heart sank. That was all, huh? It wasn't fair how much it hurt, given how low her expectations had been. "I see," she managed, after an extended pause.

"I think this was maybe a mistake," said David.

Mya didn't trust herself to reply. Even though she knew she was justified in being angry—even though she knew she could have been much worse, but hadn't—she felt partially responsible for him giving up. Again, she wondered just what he'd expected. Hugs and a mutual agreement to add each other to their Christmas card lists?

He stood up, a little unsteady on his feet, and walked out without another word. Just like that. Like she was nothing. And goddamn it all, Mya couldn't fight the tears anymore.

Chapter Ten

The day after Mya's meeting with her dad, she was in another room with throw pillows and sofas, but this time it was to meet a different man—her new counsellor, Mitch.

Mitch had a male receptionist who had shown Mya in, pointed out a place in the corner where she could get Emma settled, and given her a questionnaire to fill out while Mitch finished up paperwork somewhere else in the office. The questions were pretty standard—name, age, address—but then there was a part that asked Mya what she 'hoped to gain' from her 'counselling experience.'

She scrunched up her nose. Counselling experience? It made it sound like the world's most boring tourist attraction. Was there going to be a chance to buy souvenirs at the end?

Mya tapped the end of her pen next to the question, figuring she had to write something. *I'm hoping to… make my social worker happy by coming here, so I can prove to her I'm a good mum?* It maybe wasn't the answer they were hoping for, but it was honest.

Emma stirred in her carrier and Mya saw she'd kicked her blanket off. She got her all tucked in again and then turned to go back to her chair, surprised to see Mitch had entered without her hearing. He was just standing there, by the door, observing. *Must have the reflexes of a cat.*

Mya swallowed, uncomfortable. "Uh, hi."

"Hello," said Mitch. The tone sounded friendly, but she didn't know if it was put on. "Shall we sit?"

They sat and Mya passed him her questionnaire. Mitch set it off to the side, not even glancing at it. "So," he began, "what brings you to my office?"

Mya stammered a little bit, not sure what to say. It was basically another version of the questionnaire question, except worse because he was looking at her while she tried to answer.

Mitch smiled and stood up again. "Let's start with something simpler, shall we? Would you like a cup of tea? Some juice?"

"Juice," said Mya. Her throat did feel weirdly tight, now she thought about it.

Mitch stuck his head out of the door, gave the drinks order to his receptionist, and then sat down again. He picked up the questionnaire and Mya saw his eyes drop immediately to the last question.

"You want to be a good mum, eh? What do you think makes one of those?"

"Umm." Mya's eyes flit to the door, then back again. Her dad's words from the day before echoed in her head. *Why do I feel like I'm on trial?*

"There are no wrong answers," said Mitch, but Mya didn't quite believe him. At least twelve of them sprang to her mind, just at the suggestion, but could she think of a single *right* answer? Of course not.

"Listen," she said, "this is a bit..." Mya closed her eyes. "This is hard. I'm... I've been here like five minutes and already feel out of my depth."

"I appreciate your honesty," said Mitch. "I think it's hard for most people, especially at the start. You know, when you study counselling, they make you have a couple of sessions with someone else, first. Just to help us know what it feels like, on that side of the table."

Huh. That was actually kind of weirdly reassuring. Mya wanted to ask how it had gone, but wasn't sure if that was appropriate, and supposed that it must have been okay, if Mitch had passed his course and was now a counsellor himself.

"You know, Mya," he said, almost as if reading her thoughts, "you can ask me anything. There's no judgement here. You can tell me anything, and it'll stay confidential, except in a few circumstances."

A warning noise went off in Mya's brain. "What kind of circumstances?"

"If I thought you or someone else was in danger," Mitch said easily. "I'd have a legal responsibility to report it."

"Oh." Mya sagged in her seat, warning noise fading into the distance. "I guess that's fair."

Mitch smiled and looked at Emma, who was gurgling a little.

"Have you got kids?" Mya asked him, on impulse, again worried she was being inappropriate, but he had said she could ask *anything*.

"My husband and I are hoping to adopt," said Mitch. "It's a long process, but we're getting through it."

"Right," said Mya. "I know all about processes."

Mitch asked her what she meant and she explained the basics of what she'd experienced in the past two weeks: statements and forms, tests and waiting periods.

"Can be a lot," Mitch mused. "How are you finding it?"

Mya sighed. "Long," she answered honestly. "It's frustrating. A lot of the time, I think there's got to be simpler ways of doing things, but I don't actually know what they are."

Mitch laughed lightly. "Yes, I know what you mean."

The receptionist brought in Mya's juice and tea for Mitch. After she'd had a sip—the good kind of apple juice, made from pressed apples not just from concentrate—Mya felt a lot more relaxed. She slipped easily into talking about her dad. Honestly, she wasn't even sure how it happened. One minute, she was thanking Mitch for the drink, and the next she was recounting the terrible meeting at Jane's office.

"That must have been hard," said Mitch.

"I guess it was always gonna be," said Mya, "but it was like he didn't even try to make it better. That's why I was so mad. If he'd come in and said sorry, I might have heard him out, but he wasn't really even saying anything." She paused, knowing she could probably get away with dropping the topic and moving on to something else, but now that she'd started, Mya found that she did want to get stuff off her chest. "I've been thinking about that last time I saw him. Before yesterday," she continued.

Mitch produced a clipboard from under his chair. "Do you mind if I make a few notes?" Mya hesitated, and he reassured her that she could read them, if she wanted to. "They're just for my own use, so I don't forget anything important."

"O-okay," said Mya. It felt weird, but she figured there was no real harm. "So, um, my dad," she went on, trying to regain her train of thought. "I dreamt about it last night, and it was so real. Like I was right back there again—the house we lived in at the time. Mum moved, after dad left. I'm not sure how long after. It feels like it was a long time, but being five…" She shrugged, suppressing a shiver, and Mitch smiled encouragingly.

"Time moves slowly when you're really young, but I guess that doesn't matter. The bit that gets me is that we didn't know it was the last time we were gonna see him. He didn't tell us he was moving out, he just…" A lump caught in her throat, and she took another sip of juice.

"He never came home. Sometimes I wonder if he'd said anything to mum, but I don't know. She wouldn't talk about it. Zhara kept asking where dad was, and when he was coming back, and mum would either get a strange look on her face and go quiet, or just leave the room. Sometimes… sometimes I heard her crying. I told Zhara to stop asking her, because I didn't want mum to be sad. But Zhara… I think she took it harder than me." Mya shook her head. "No. Zhara *definitely* took it harder than me. She was thirteen and I think she understood more. She didn't stop trying to talk to mum. Said she had a right to know. That we both did. But after a while, I think I was scared of the answer. We wondered, maybe, if he'd died. But Zhara eventually said no, if that was the case, we'd definitely have been told. She'd even looked through newspaper announcements in the library, just to check, but there was never anything."

Mya looked up, suddenly coming back to herself. She hadn't realized she'd been talking for so long, and felt a little embarrassed, but Mitch didn't look annoyed.

"You said you were…" He paused. "Five, is that right?" Mya nodded. "There's eight years between you and your sister?"

Mya smiled a little wryly. "It never really feels like it, but yeah. We spent all our time together. She was my best friend, until Kian… well." She contemplated taking more juice, but she'd been holding the glass and her palms had warmed it up, so it wasn't so nice anymore. *No distraction there, might as well get on with it.*

"Mum was alone for four years before she met Kian, and then it was like everything changed overnight. That weird time thing again, I guess? It was probably more like weeks, maybe a couple of months. Everything seemed fine at first. You always see kids in movies react badly to their parents finding new people, but I guess it didn't seem that weird to me. Maybe I just didn't think about it. But Zhara actually really liked Kian. At the time, I thought she was excited to replace dad or whatever, and I didn't blame her. Then, when I grew up a bit more and looked back on it… I think she might have actually had a crush on Kian. I…" Mya looked up at Mitch and swallowed. "Is it weird if I think it was both?"

Mitch tilted his head in a noncommittal kind of way. "It's not my place to judge," he reiterated.

"Right," said Mya. "Well, anyway. Everything seemed fine for a while. Mum and Zhara were happy, and I was happy for them. But then—and this part actually did happen overnight, I'm pretty sure—I came home from school and Mum was crying again. 'No,' she kept telling Kian, 'no, she doesn't have to go. This doesn't have to happen!'

"Turns out, she'd told him that she wasn't Zhara's real mum—that my dad had her with someone else, and Mum had just taken over raising her when they got together—and Kian decided that meant Zhara didn't belong with us. He said he didn't want someone else's brat living under his roof, so he told her to get out. Just like that. Zhara hadn't even known about the mum thing."

Mya wiped at a tear that had escaped down her cheek. "Zhara was so… broken. In shock, I think, at first. Kian didn't give her any time to process, or find anywhere to go. She had to pack a bag and get out that night. I kept expecting her to scream, or cry, but she didn't. She…" Mya shook her head, changing tack. "Mum kept begging Kian, but he wouldn't listen. Eventually, he snapped at her and she stopped. His house, his rules, he kept saying. But it was mum's house. The place we'd moved to after dad left. Kian and Mum weren't even married, at that point. I couldn't understand any of it, and no one would explain it to me."

Mya had been about to continue—it felt like she'd cracked open her soul, and suddenly everything was pouring out—but she caught Mitch's eye, and something in his expression made her pause again. She sniffed and he offered her a tissue.

"I'm sorry, Mya, but our time's up for today."

"Oh." She felt her cheeks burn and rubbed at her eyes, resigning herself to the fact that she must look like more of a disaster than usual.

"I know it probably seems unfair to stop here," said Mitch. "Unkind, even. But all of these things weigh heavy on us, and you'll probably find yourself feeling a little unbalanced after taking the weight off your shoulders. It's for you as much as everyone not to try and do it all in one go. Counselling helps most people, but sometimes it gets harder before it's easier. You need to give it time."

"Sure," Mya mumbled. Emma was stirring again and she was glad of the distraction. Mya lifted her and left without looking at either Mitch or his secretary again.

Jane had offered to pick them up, but Mya had said she wanted to walk back. She'd imagined wanting fresh air to try and clear her mind, but when she got outside it was exactly like Mitch had said. She felt off kilter, like she'd been spun in circles, and was more tired than after she'd given birth, even. So she called Jane and got a lift after all.

Back in the Mother and Baby Unit, Mya fed Emma, changed and burped her, and then all but collapsed on her bed, not even bothering to change into her nightdress.

***

There was crying. Mya turned toward the sound of it, expecting to see Emma, but she found herself looking at her mum. She was pleading with Kian not to kick Zhara out again. He stood over her, and she cowered, until she was almost crumpled against the wall. Kian reached past her for the fire poker and lifted it above his head. Mya heard herself gasp, and then he turned around, fast as a snake. His eyes bored into hers and she felt herself cowering just like her mum.

Mya glanced off to the side, to where her mum had been, but she couldn't see her anymore. Anything that wasn't

Kian had darkened in the corners of her vision, and all she could focus on was the looming mass of him as he came closer.

Kian grinned and lifted the poker higher still.

Mya screwed her eyes shut, bracing herself for the blow, but then there was a noise pulling at her attention. Different from the earlier crying. Screaming?

She woke in a jolt, her heart hammering and breaths coming in short bursts. Fucking hell, it was the fucking fire alarms. *Again!* She lay back on the bed, needing to catch her breath, and then made her way over to Emma, who was indeed screaming.

Everything in Mya's head was scrambled, and she found herself glad that she hadn't brought up anything else during her counselling session, if it was going to turn into literal nightmare fuel.

As pissed off as she was with whoever kept triggering the fire alarms, Mya couldn't decide if the rude awakening was preferable to her dreams.

Chapter Eleven

Mya spent an hour of Sunday morning uselessly googling her mum, trying both her maiden and married surnames. For the lack of results, it shouldn't have taken more than ten minutes, but her phone was 'borrowing' WiFi from the upstairs flat, which had an unsecured connection. It was patchy and kept cutting out, and although there were a couple of similar names on family tree websites, none of them were exactly right, and all the really helpful details were behind paywalls.

Just as Mya was about to close the browser and start thinking about breakfast, she decided to search for something else. 'Jaundice in adults' she typed in and scrolled, her heart sinking the further down the page she travelled. The words 'serious,' 'late stage,' and 'liver failure' jumped out at her, alongside a bit about alcoholism as the main cause.

Mya closed her eyes, her appetite suddenly gone, and sat with that a minute: the possibility that her dad might die, sooner rather than later. She felt sadness replace the anger she'd felt when she'd seen him. Had that really been the last time? For good this time? Should she have put her feelings aside and tried harder to be nice to him?

She felt hollow and imagined a great big pit in her stomach, opening to turn in on itself. It made her feel nauseated, her head spinning like it had done when she'd come out of her counselling appointment.

Get a grip, she told herself, and forced a deep breath, holding it for a moment. Just as she was starting to feel right-side up again, the phone buzzed in her hand and she jumped, her heart leaping.

Zhara's name glowed on the screen.

Mya pressed 'accept call' and took another breath. "Hey."

"You okay?"

"Yeah," she lied.

Zhara made a disbelieving sound, but didn't call her on it. "What's up? You left me, like, ten messages."

Mya had left her exactly three, but she returned the favour of not correcting her sister. Rather than dive into what was actually bothering her, which she could barely process for herself, let alone contemplate trying to break to Zhara, she focused on practicalities.

"Weird question, but do you remember mum having a sister?"

There was silence on the other end of the line, and Mya had to pull it away from her ear to check the screen and see if it was still connected. It was. "Zhara?"

"I'm thinking," she said, and stayed silent a while longer. Mya waited, glad that Zhara was the one paying for the call. When Zhara spoke again, her voice was so quiet Mya barely recognised it. "I don't remember a lot from back then."

"When?" Mya asked, wondering if she meant before their dad left, or when Kian came.

"Any of it," said Zhara. "Kristen says I must have blocked it all out."

Mya blinked. *Kristen?* "Who's Kristen?"

Zhara cleared her throat and Mya imagined herself literally shaking the topic away. "Anyway," she said, pointedly not answering the question, "yeah. I… I'm not sure."

Mya frowned. She couldn't imagine just having forgotten everything they'd been through—it was etched in her brain like stone, a great big mountain that made a shadow she could never quite step outside of—but she supposed not everyone was like her.

If Zhara *did* know something, deep down, Mya wanted to uncover it. She thought of what David had said. "Does the name 'Mouse' mean anything to you?"

Zhara laughed suddenly. "God, yeah. Wow, I haven't heard that in years."

Mya sat further up in bed. From her new vantage point, she saw Emma's eyes twitch, like she was about to open them and start wailing for another feed. Mya crossed her fingers, hoping she'd hold off a little while longer, at least until she'd finished her call, and Emma mercifully let out a little snore. "So, who is Mouse?"

"Aunt Minnie," said Zhara easily, like it made sense.

Mya stared at the phone for a moment, waiting for further explanation. Then, "Minnie Mouse? Are you taking the piss?" she asked when nothing was forthcoming.

Zhara laughed again. It was kind of nice to hear. "Mouse was just what Dad called her. I think because she hated it. Mum told you and me to call her Aunt Minnie, but her real name was something else. Ghanaian, probably, like Mum's. Except harder to say, or spell. You know how a lot of immigrants adopt an anglicised name when they move here."

Okay, yeah, that part made sense. "But what do you mean her name is 'probably' Ghanaian?"

"I dunno," said Zhara, her mirth having worn off and tone returning to her usual tired exasperation. "Parents get their kids to call adults auntie and uncle all the time. I don't know if Minnie and Mum were actually sisters. Could be, though."

This was brilliant. Mya still didn't have a full name to work with, but she felt a step closer to figuring it out. "No," she told Zhara, happy to fill in the blank for her, too. "Dad definitely said she was Mum's sister."

The line went deathly silent again.

"Zhara?"

"Did you say Dad?"

"I…" *Shit.* She had.

"You were talking to Dad?" Zhara pressed. "When?"

"Uh…"

"Mya, don't you dare lie to me."

She bit her lip and admitted, "Thursday."

Zhara swore. "You saw him? In person?" she asked, but before Mya could answer, she went on a rant about betrayal and abandonment and, "How could you, Mya?" she kept repeating.

"Whoa!" She'd expected Zhara to be unhappy hearing about the meeting, but her real reaction felt excessive. "Calm down."

"Calm down?" echoed Zhara, her voice louder than ever. "You want me to calm down? Fuck you, Mya!"

And then there was silence again. When Mya checked her screen, she saw Zhara had hung up. She didn't know what to do—if she should give her time to cool off or call her straight back, but then Emma woke up for real and that settled it, Mya would have to deal with her sister's latest meltdown later.

***

On Monday, Jane came around with the news that the police had interviewed Ryan about the text he'd sent and let him off with a warning.

90

"He denied sending the other one," Jane explained, "and they couldn't find any evidence to indicate it was him."

Mya groaned. She'd rationalised at the time that it worked against her for the first text not to have been from Kian, but to now know that there were two people out there wanting to harass her felt like too much. Yes, she'd screwed up and made some awful decisions, but she still didn't deserve that.

"How do you feel?" asked Jane.

"Annoyed," said Mya. "Pissed off. Like I want to punch a wall. Pick one."

Jane set down her mug. "Mya…"

"No." Mya stood up, too agitated to sit down and enjoy a cup of tea. "This is bullshit. We all know who sent the first text and no one's doing anything!"

"The police need evidence," said Jane, reasonably.

"I'm sure if they searched the house, they'd find it," Mya shot back.

"And it would get thrown out of court if it ever got that far," said Jane. "I'm sorry, but that's not how it works."

Mya scoffed. "*Does* it work? The police need evidence before they can go in and look for evidence? That doesn't even make sense."

Jane didn't say anything to that, so Mya reached for the next thing on her agenda.

"Mum has a sister, apparently. Can you get the police to look her up?"

"I can put out feelers," said Jane, "but I can't guarantee–"

"You didn't seem to have any problems finding my dad," said Mya. The words came out like an accusation, and her voice was raised, but she didn't care. Why did Zhara get to be the one to let off steam while Mya had to just accept all the shit fired at her?

"As one of your legal guardians," Jane tried again, voice still annoyingly calm, "I had to do due diligence in letting him know what had happened to you."

"Fat lot of good that did.".

"And the police have already spoken to your mother," Jane reminded her. "She's not officially missing."

"Fuck what's official!"

Jane leaned away from Mya and she let out a long breath, unclenching her fists.

"I'm sorry," said Mya. "I know I shouldn't explode at you—I know it's not your fault—but it's not fair!"

"It's not," agreed Jane. They sat in silence for a long moment, then Jane said she had other visits to make.

Fine, thought Mya. She could make visits too. If she needed to take actions into her own hands, she would. She could have tried the crappy upstairs internet again, but wanted to get out of the flat, so headed to the local library.

The cold spring air helped calm Mya down further, and thankfully she still had her library card in her school bag——one of the few things she hadn't lost. It was tricky finding a seat in the computer room that had space to place Emma's carrier beside her, but she'd just managed it when a librarian came along and tapped her shoulder.

"Excuse me."

Mya glanced up. "Yes?"

"Excuse me, what age are you?"

Mya stopped typing in her borrower number and gave the woman her full attention. "What?"

"Well," she looked at Emma briefly, then back to Mya, frowning, "it's just you look under eighteen."

"Is that a problem?" Mya asked through gritted teeth. Of all the places she expected to get shit for being a teen mum, the library wasn't one of them.

"Under-eighteens need to use the children's computer suite," said the woman.

Mya sighed. *Seriously?* "I'm sixteen. Does it actually matter?"

"Rules are rules," said the librarian primly.

Mya sighed again and rubbed her forehead. "Fine." She let the woman lead her to the children's computers, trying valiantly to ignore all the nine-year-olds staring at her. When she got logged in, it took Mya a minute to figure out what she should search for this time.

'What is Minnie short for?' she typed, disheartened to read that it was a nickname that could be applied to literally any name beginning with 'M.'

'Female Ghanaian names beginning with 'M.'' she typed next, disappointed that, according to the top result, there only seemed to be one of them. That couldn't be right, could it? The list had about thirty that began with the letter 'A.'

Mya looked again at her single 'M' result and smiled. *Mawusi.* That had to be it, didn't it? She opened a new tab and searched for Mawusi Gyasi, hoping that her aunt hadn't gotten married or changed her surname.

The page was slow in loading, but then there it was, someone with that name not only alive and living in England, but in the same town. Mya stared at the online phone book result. She couldn't believe it was a coincidence—what were the chances of that?—but it was almost as hard to imagine she had an aunt living so close and had no idea all this time. Had she ever met her? What age had she been? Mya didn't have to wonder why her mum and aunt had lost touch, at least. Kian had cut Akosua off from everyone. Sometimes, Mya thought he'd even succeeded in cutting her off from herself. But she could muse on that later, once she'd actually found her. She scribbled down the address on the back of her hand and set off, hoping against hope.

***

The house Mya found was small but neat, with a short front lawn, clean windows, and none of the random rubbish tossed around by the wind that a lot of other gardens in the street had.

The gate didn't squeak as Mya opened it, and the doorbell seemed to work.

She held her breath but didn't have to wait long. Within moments someone had opened up, demanding to know what she wanted and why she was there.

Mya gaped a little at the woman—partially at how brusque she was, but also because of how startling the resemblance was. It was so obvious they were sisters. Mawusi didn't just look like Akosua, she was the image of what Akosua *used* to be, before she got painfully thin and her hair started falling out. Mya might as well have been looking at a ghost. She wondered how Zhara could have ever doubted the biological link, but she'd been young and Mya supposed you didn't always think too much about the people you're used to seeing.

"Well, what do you want?" Mawusi pressed.

"My mum," said Mya, realising she should have planned in advance what she was going to say.

Mawusi's eyes got huge and she looked up and down the street, like she expected to see someone hiding in the shadows. "Go away! Go on, get out of here!" Her accent got stronger when infused with her obvious distress, and again it took Mya aback, giving her a sense of déjà vu. That was how her mum used to speak, before Kian insisted she try and speak "normal" and she started forcing an English accent. Before he got her to stop talking almost entirely.

"Is she here?" Mya tried again. "Akosua. Is she–?"

Mawusi tried to shut the door in her face, but Mya stuck out her foot, jamming it in the small space between the frame and the door. It hurt, but she couldn't allow herself to focus on the pain.

"Listen, I'm not trying to–"

Mawusi backed up a little bit and Mya saw further past her into the hall, her eyes landing on a suitcase at the foot of the stairs that she'd recognise anywhere. It had a vibrant floral design that Akosua had made the mistake of admiring, once. Mya had been with her mum the day a really pushy vendor in the market pressured her into buying it. Kian had hit the roof when she brought it home, going on and on about her wasting his money, and of course it never got used—at least until now.

Mya felt her blood leap in her veins at the realisation that she'd done it—she'd actually found her mum—but then she looked back at Mawusi and saw her expression wasn't that of someone who'd given in, or been convinced. She was shaking, holding a hand to her mouth, and sneaking glances at the phone on the hall table.

Oh my god, she thinks I'm gonna seriously hurt her. Horror flooded through Mya and she wanted to fix the whole situation—find a way to put her aunt at ease, and talk to her mum—but it dawned on her how she must look to Mawusi. Desperate. Crazed. Maybe even unhinged. None of the descriptors were entirely wrong. *Does that make me the bad guy here? I'm acting more like Kian than someone who just needs to see her mum.*

"Please," Mya tried again, removing her foot from the door. "I'm sorry for scaring you, I just need to–"

Mawusi jolted forward the second Mya was out of the way and slammed the door shut. Mya stared at the dark wood, a little stunned. She considered knocking again, or shouting through the letterbox, but figured it was too late.

She'd found her mum, but it was increasingly clear her mum didn't want to be found.

Ellie Rose McKee

Chapter Twelve

The frustration Mya felt over getting so close to reaching her mum only to fall at the last hurdle grew ever bigger with each step on her walk home. She figured that she'd have to sleep on it and decide later if it was a total lost cause or there might be some way to salvage it another day—she'd come so far, it seemed wrong to turn away completely—but practicalities were in the back of her mind. For the most part, her brain was stuck on replaying the scene, hearing the words and feeling the feelings.

The sharp bite of rejection. The anger at herself for leaving herself open to be hurt again. The disappointment that Zhara had been right about their mum and their dad both, meaning Mya trying to reach them had driven a wedge between her and her sister for nothing.

Mya expected to be in a rotten mood at least until she'd gotten that much-needed sleep—but then she turned the corner and stopped dead at the sight of Richard standing in the courtyard of the Mother and Baby Unit.

He was gazing at the upstairs windows and didn't notice her at first, so she stole a moment to just take him in. Then the gate creaked under her hand and the spell was broken. Rich looked down, his face snapping in an instant from bored to alert. Wary, even. Uncertain.

They stood frozen for a minute, just continuing the mutual stare, until he tilted his head a little.

"You okay?"

Mya's feet started moving of their own accord and her heart began hammering in her ears. Skipping several gears, her body left its autopilot setting and slammed into a weird hyper-aware state as she reached for Richard and he opened his arms in response. Mya felt the cool flesh of his bare forearms against her own, smelt the musk of his deodorant, and felt the damp on her cheeks from her own leaking eyes.

He was there. Right there! And he was real.

Mya figured a similar kind of autopilot was going on with Rich, because she felt the moment he seemed to notice it. He kept hugging her, but there was a slight shift in his posture.

"No," she told him, firm as she could make it sound through a running nose.

Richard made a sound that seemed unsure if it was supposed to be a laugh or a sigh. "What do you mean, no?" He went to pull away, but Mya locked her arms more tightly around him.

"Don't."

"Mya."

"No," she said again. "I need you." Her tears were still coming, but more slowly. Mya barely knew what she was saying, just that she had to say it. "Richard."

He unhooked her arms from around his neck and looked in her eyes. A soul gaze that made her shiver. "What happened?"

Rejection bit again. Deeper. Mya heard herself laugh––it was definitely a laugh, but it sounded strangled. "You don't remember? You left me."

"Mya…"

She snatched her hands out of his, embarrassed that she'd wanted to keep holding onto him, like an idiot. *Am I ever gonna learn to stop reaching for people?* "Did you really come here just so we could keep saying each other's names?"

Richard leaned away, as if she'd slapped him. "Are you mad at me?"

Mya scoffed, crossing her arms. "Oh, couldn't you tell?"

His eyes narrowed. "I thought I was the one who got to be pissed off."

"You don't have a monopoly on it."

Rich gaped a little. "Mya, you didn't tell me you were *pregnant*. You didn't trust me. That's huge!"

"Yes, it's huge!" She was yelling now, her tears having rebounded with a vengeance, but fuck it, this had been coming long enough. "I tried to tell you. I did, I tried. But you broke up with me, Rich. You broke up with me and—" She choked a sob, but couldn't stop.

"I was off with you for, what? Like two weeks? Three?" Mya continued. "I had big things going on, that I had to get my head around, and rather than wait, or fucking warn me how serious things were—that you wanted to take a break if we couldn't sort them out—you just jumped to the breaking up. *Bam!* Like that. And then there was no talking. At all. You remember avoiding me in the halls? Because I do. I do, Richard. It fucking hurt, and I tried! I—"

Mya broke off as her tears finally overwhelmed her. Her breath was coming in short bursts that didn't leave her quite enough air, and her nose was still blocked with snot, but she couldn't think for long enough to remember in which pocket of her repurposed school bag she'd put the tissues she always kept for Emma and—Emma. Mya looked over at where she'd set down her carrier, just a few feet away, when she'd launched herself into Richard's arms.

Emma was staring back at her, her eyes wide and mouth held in a little 'o' shape. Mya went over to her, picking her up and holding her against her chest, rocking gently until her feet felt like they were back on solid ground. It took a while, and when she looked up, Mya expected Richard to be gone, but he was still there. Staring.

Mya swallowed and took a step forward. "This is Emma."

Richard blinked, his eyes clouded with a thousand different shades of emotion. "Wow. She's…"

"Big?" asked Mya. She'd seemed so small, initially, and then had lost some weight in the first couple of days after being born, but since then it was like she was on growth hormones. Which, maybe she was, given all of the things Mya's milk was supposed to have in it.

Rich smiled, his eyes not leaving Emma. "Real, I was gonna say."

"Oh." Mya felt herself blush, and felt foolish for it—because seriously, what did she have to be shy about?—but it was what it was. And it beat arguing. Mya took a deep breath. "I'm sorry I bit your head off."

Rich didn't say it was okay, but did ask if Mya wanted to go for a walk, to "talk it out now," which she figured amounted to the same thing.

She nodded and they set off, only to have to pause when they got to the gate, because only one could go through at a time. Rich gestured Mya ahead, then held out his arm in a silent offer to take Emma's carrier. Mya gently placed Emma, who was now sleeping, back inside and handed her over, watching Richard closer than ever as he walked slowly along the canal path.

They hadn't verbally decided on a destination, but it warmed Mya that they apparently both had the same instinct to go towards the park.

"So, you called," Rich began conversationally.

"You hung up," Mya replied, and he winced. "I'm sorry, I didn't mean it to come out like that. I wasn't having a go—or another go—I just–"

"I'd just gotten out of an exam," said Rich. "You know how you're not supposed to have phones on you, but no one really listens? I'd only forgotten to turn the bloody sound off."

"Oh, shit!" said Mya, her hand going to her mouth. That was bad. Really, really bad. She'd heard stories of whole exam halls getting their papers scrapped over stuff like that. "What happened?"

"Mr Daniels heard it and got me pulled into the Principal's office. They made me show them there weren't any text messages with notes, or whatever, and that the internet was off. Gave me an official warning and said if it happened again, I could kiss my results goodbye."

Mya shook her head. It was a lucky escape, but still pretty bad. The teachers must be watching Rich like a hawk during the rest of his exams. As if there wasn't already so much pressure on him! "I'm so sorry. I didn't think. I've been so caught up with..." She gestured to Emma. "GCSEs completely slipped off my radar."

"Hey," Richard said softly. He reached for her hand with his free one and held it for a second, until Mya's gaze met his, and he let go again. "I, uh, wasn't having a go either."

They lapsed into silence, then something occurred to Mya. "How did you know where I was?"

"Jane gave me the address. She said you wouldn't mind."

"I don't!" exclaimed Mya, louder than she intended. "I, uh." She cleared her throat and lowered her voice, ignoring the cute way Rich was smiling out one corner of his mouth. "I mean, of course I don't mind. Wait." She paused again. "Are you and Jane in regular contact?"

She'd known she'd spoken to him and his parents at least once, when Emma was first born, but hadn't known it was more than that. Mya had actually figured Jane would have dropped contact when he said he'd needed time, like how the police hadn't kept chasing her mum. *I might need to actually get over that at some point.*

"She's my social worker, too," said Rich, making Mya's eyebrows go up. "Or, Emma's, technically. So mine by extension. I guess I wouldn't still be on her books if I'd chosen to walk away."

Mya bit her lip. "What made you walk back?" she asked tentatively. "Now, I mean."

Richard frowned a little. "It was Ryan, actually."

"Huh?"

Rich shook his head. "After the exam thing, a rumour went around school that I was gonna get kicked out. Ryan heard, and he was pissed, so he sent you that text. I didn't hear about it until after the police had cautioned him. Ryan said they told him you'd been getting other threatening texts, but he swears he didn't send them. That was when I finally used my giant head to figure out something else was going on, and maybe you had a reason for not telling me about Emma." His eyes drifted down to look at her again, and he smiled with his whole mouth. "It's a nice name. I used to call my grandma–"

"I know," said Mya. "That's why I picked it." Rich blinked back at her, his mouth forming the same perfect 'o' that Emma had displayed.

Mya had to look away, just to curb her instinct to kiss him. "Your head isn't giant," she said instead, making him laugh.

"Tell that to my dad. Every time he wants to buy me a baseball cap, he has to get my size ordered in specially."

Mya grinned. "Maybe it's a little big," she allowed, "but not, like, super giant. Just Richard-sized. Perfectly in proportion to the rest of you."

Richard winked and she felt her cheeks flame. "God, I didn't mean it like that!"

He shook his head, but was doing the half-smile thing again. This time when they slipped into silence, it was comfortable. Mya hated to break it, but she knew they couldn't just leave things there. Not when there was still so much to sort out.

They came to the little gate to the park and Richard held it open, allowing Mya to walk in ahead of him again. She went over to the first free bench and sat, exhausted by the emotional weight of the day. The year, even.

"So," she began.

"So," agreed Richard, placing Emma's carrier on the ground between them. "Can I ask about the texts? About what else you had going on?"

Mya filled her lungs slowly and fixed her gaze on a seagull in the distance, knowing it was the only way she could get it out. No matter how many times she talked about it, it didn't get any easier. Not until after.

"I wasn't safe. A-at home. My step-dad... if he'd found out, I was scared he might kill me. As in, literally. And then, when he did find out..."

Richard blew a breath out through his teeth. He took a minute to consider his words, but rather than ask about Kian, he said, "And today?"

Mya frowned. "What do you mean?"

"You were upset today. Just now, before you saw me. Did something else happen? More texts?"

Ah, so he wanted to get it all out in one go before reacting. She could respect that—even if she didn't really want to get into it. Mya figured she'd just have to get over her discomfort and cough up more honesty. She owed Rich that.

"I've been trying to find my mum," she admitted. "I think I actually did find her, but didn't get to talk to her. I'm not, uh–" Her voice cracked a little. "I don't think she wants to see me. You caught me just as that was sinking in."

She saw Rich nodding from the corner of her eye and turned her face more towards him.

"Are you safe now? In the Mother and Baby place?"

"For now," said Mya. "I don't think I'll feel really safe until Kian is behind bars, but..." She trailed off again, smiling a little as she thought of her weird housemates, that she'd already grown fond of. Even Bernice. "It's not a bad place."

Emma started to stir and Rich smiled down at her. "What about you, eh? You like it there?"

"You can hold her," said Mya, not sure if she was pushing too far, too fast. "I-if you want."

Richard looked terrified, suddenly. "What if I break her?"

"You?" said Mya, genuinely surprised. "I remember seeing that photo of you with your sisters right after they were born, and there were two of them!"

"I know," said Rich. "I just... it's different. She..." He shook his head a little. "She's *mine*."

Mya's heart flipped. "You'll be fine," she assured Rich, only to find her own hands shaking and weirdly numb as she took Emma out of her carrier and handed her over.

Richard cradled her, his face filled with awe—for all of two minutes until Emma either spontaneously filled her nappy or caught a whiff of a scent she wasn't used to and realised she was being held by someone unfamiliar. She screwed her eyes shut, opened her mouth wide, and wailed.

Mya winced and prepared herself to take Emma back, but Richard didn't look all that put off. He seemed in his element, now that he was actually holding her.

"Oh, hush now," he whispered, "you'll be goin' back to your mum in a minute. Just let me see you."

Emma didn't take the slightest notice and Richard eventually sighed and handed her back.

"She is due a feed," said Mya, standing up.

"You breastfeeding?" asked Richard, then his eyes went wide. "Sorry, that was personal."

Mya felt her earlier blush return and deepen. "I don't mind you being personal," she said quietly, biting her lip.

They began walking the short distance back to the park entrance only to pause when Emma stopped crying almost as swiftly as she'd started. Both Rich and Mya watched her as she gazed up at the tree over their heads, mesmerised.

"You know," said Rich, "my sisters were just the same. When Dad couldn't get them to settle in the house, he had to go outside and rock them under a tree. Worked like a charm."

Mya laughed. "Really? What if it was raining?"

"Well, umbrellas are a thing," Rich pointed out. "Tilt them just right and you can still see the trees and not get soaked."

Mya cringed, because of course that was the obvious answer to a stupid question, but her shoulders relaxed at the easy back and forth. "Listen, did I mention I'm sorry? About the not-telling-you thing?"

"You did," affirmed Richard. "I don't think I actually said sorry for my part in it, but I am. I... god, it sounds awful, but I had it in my head you'd found someone else. Didn't think I could bear you dumping me, so I got in there first."

Mya groaned. "My sister said that. She's so gonna gloat that she was right."

Richard gave her a quizzical look. "Weird thing to gloat about."

She waved a hand. "You don't know Zhara. Weird about covers it."

They walked a little further on, back in comfortable silence until they were on the canal path again, just around the corner from the Mother and Baby Unit.

"Listen," said Rich, "I know we've still got a ways to go, but..." He trailed off.

"Yeah?" Mya prompted.

"Are we good?" he asked. "For now, I mean? We can talk again?"

"Sure," said Mya, amazed at her own ability to sound so casual when her insides were freaking out. "What about seeing you again?" she asked at the same time Rich said, "Maybe I can come back another day?"

They laughed, then, "yeah," said Mya. "I'd like that."

"Good," said Rich. His own voice was quietly calm, but his eyes were sparkling. He looked down at Emma, who had yet again drifted back to sleep, and reached out to lightly stroke her hair. "She is beautiful."

"She is," agreed Mya, her mouth splitting in a grin.

"There's a lot to figure out."

"Yup."

Mya wanted to say more—to tell him she loved him, and missed him, and despite everything was glad that they had Emma—but it had been too long since either of them had used the L-word, and everything between them was still so fragile. So she watched as he took back his hand, looked up from Emma, smiled a smile that was just for her, and then set off on his walk home.

Chapter Thirteen

Mya spent the rest of the week so visibly uplifted from Richard's visit, Lynne said it was starting to freak her out. It didn't matter how many times Mya's sleep was disturbed by the fire alarms randomly going off, or how over the top Bernice was being, everything was fine because Richard didn't hate her. He'd said he wanted to see her again. *And* he seemed as taken with Emma as Mya herself was.

Lynne's teasing didn't take off the shine one bit.

Of course Mya still had brief moments mired with grief over her mother's rejection, but every time one hit, she would close her eyes, remember Rich's face as he watched Emma, and the sting softened.

"Someone's happy," said Mitch as Mya walked into her Friday afternoon counselling appointment.

She set Emma's carrier in the corner of the room, away from both drafts and direct heat, and settled herself in her seat. "I'm good."

"Any particular reason?" asked Mitch.

"My–" She caught herself just in time, not wanting to jinx it. "Emma's dad. He came to see me. *Us.* And it went well. I couldn't actually have imagined it going better."

"Wow," said Mitch, clearly impressed. "Why don't you tell me about it?"

Mya detailed the entire exchange, which transitioned into her talking about how they'd gotten together. "We went to the same primary school," she was explaining. "Our birthdays are only a few days apart, but because of where they fall, I was in the school year ahead. I hadn't noticed Rich at all until I had to repeat my last year and we ended up in the same class. A group of us were friends, but Rich and I really hit it off."

"That's a long time to be together, for someone so young," said Mitch.

"Well, yeah. But we didn't actually become a couple until we'd started high school. There were a weird few months where Richard would alternate between being super nice, and then ignoring me completely."

Mitch nodded knowingly. "Teenage boy mixed signals. I think I remember them."

Mya laughed. "Yeah, something like that. I don't think he was doing it on purpose, he was as confused as I was. But I eventually called him out on it. He denied it, of course, but when I pressed, he asked me out."

Mitch attached a fresh sheet of paper to his clipboard. "How did that go?"

Mya pulled a face. "The first time? Not so well. I thought he was joking."

"So you laughed," said Mitch.

Mya sighed. "I laughed. And then he got upset and said he hadn't meant it anyway, which was when I realised it wasn't actually a joke. I tried to talk to him, but he kept avoiding me. For, like, weeks. And we were in the same class!" She shook her head. "Eventually, he cooled off and we started talking again, though it was so awkward. I kept waiting for him to ask me again, and when he didn't then, well…" She shrugged.

Mitch looked up, his pen poised on his notes. "What?"

"I, um." Mya bit her lip. "I kissed him." Mitch smiled and she was quick to add, "It was just a peck! Enough to tell him I maybe liked him too. Rich looked so startled, I almost laughed again. But I held back, and then he asked me if I wanted to go to the movies that weekend. We've been together ever since. Or…" Mya glanced at Emma, then faltered a little.

"It's so weird. We've kind of always been solid. I mean, six years! It blows my mind sometimes. Or it did. When I got pregnant, I stupidly didn't expect things to change. I mean, obviously once I found out, I expected a baby, but…" She shook her head. "I don't think I'm explaining this right."

"Take your time," said Mitch, and she took a breath.

"I think what I'm trying to say is that I figured we'd always stay together. No matter what. It felt safe. And I'm so mad at myself for ruining it. It didn't even occur to me that we'd break up. I guess because I knew Rich wasn't the kind of guy to do that, if I told him. I just hadn't planned on not telling him." Mya rubbed her forehead. "It just became a giant mess so fast. And seeing him again... part of me hopes we can get back to where we were, but I don't know. Hoping now feels kinda scary."

"There's nothing to say you have to get back to how you were right away," said Mitch. "Maybe, together, you can build a relationship that's even more solid than it was before. You certainly have honesty going for you, now."

"Yeah," said Mya quietly. "I hope so." *There's that word again.*

"So," said Mitch, briefly glancing at the wall clock. Mya followed his gaze and saw they still had half a session left.

"Go on," he prompted.

Mya blinked at him. "Go on where? That's pretty much it."

Mitch leaned forward, dropping his pen in his lap so he could steeple his fingers in front of him. "So far, you've told me about your parents, your sister, and your boyfriend." Mya went to interject that Rich wasn't technically her boyfriend again yet, but Mitch held up a hand.

"When are you going to tell me about *you*?"

Mya frowned. "Me?"

Mitch nodded and Mya paused to think about it. "I don't know what to say," was literally all she could come up with. *Nice one, Mya. Ground-breaking.*

"Tell me something that's just something you know about," said Mitch. "About what happened, and how you felt. A memory."

When Mya continued to stare at him, he said, "You mentioned something about being held back a year." He glanced at his notes. "You had to repeat your last year of primary school. Why was that?"

Mya looked down at her hands, surprised to see her knuckles had gone kind of white from holding onto each other so tight. She hadn't even noticed herself doing it.

"Difficult one?" asked Mitch, and she nodded. "We don't have to, if you don't feel ready."

"No," said Mya. "I should probably just get it over with." Now that it had been pointed out, it was super obvious that she'd been holding back; ignoring the whole reason she was there. Which, it turned out, was not just so she could prove to Jane that she was willing to do what she asked and show herself responsible, or whatever it was she'd initially thought. No, the counselling was Mya's. For herself. It might make her a better mum, as a side effect, but mostly she just needed to…

110

be okay on her own? Yeah, that seemed right. And kind of felt like a breakthrough in itself, but Mitch was still looking at her expectantly.

She closed her eyes and thought back, instinctively shivering. "So, I was ten. It was a really cold winter—I mean *really* cold—more snow than I've ever seen, before or since. A lot of parents kept their kids off school, but Kian said I had to go in. He didn't want me hanging around the house and bothering him, apparently.

"I was used to walking to school on my own by then. My mum stopped taking me when Kian made her scared to leave the house. But that day, with all the snow, it seemed to take forever. I kept slipping, but eventually made it. I'd missed the 9am bell, but it didn't matter. The school was sending home the kids that had managed to get there. They said a pipe froze, or burst, or something."

When she opened her eyes, Mitch nodded encouragingly at her and Mya took a breath. "One of the teachers stood with me while they called the house, but no one answered. After they tried a couple of times, they decided to give me a lift. She—the teacher, I can't remember her name––offered to go inside and explain why I was back, but I said no. I expected Kian to be mad at me for it, but it would have been worse if I let someone else in the house.

"I went through the back door on my own—we always use the back door, I don't know why—and the first thing I saw was the phone cord ripped out of the wall. I knew then that Kian was having one of his bad days. That something had set him off. It could even have been as little as the phone ringing when he didn't expect it."

Mya shuddered, because this was getting to the really hard part, but Mitch didn't rush her. She was glad of that. "I thought I could just sneak up to my room and stay quiet until it was my normal time to be home," she continued. "But when I stepped further into the kitchen, I heard shouting. Kian's voice, screaming at my mum to get up. I heard a noise. I... I think he kicked her, because she grunted and swore. Mum never swore."

Mya shook her head. She felt cold all over, and kind of wanted to throw up. "I followed the noise into the hall to see if she was okay, and Kian was standing over her. Ever since he let his mask slip that first time and kicked Zhara out, he'd been mean. Always yelling and criticising. But that was… was…"

"Take your time," Mitch advised for the second time that day, as Mya's breath caught. He handed her the box of tissues.

"Thanks." She took one to blow her nose, and shredded another one between her fingers, which somehow helped. Mya had to close her eyes again before finishing the story.

"It was the first time I saw him hit her," she went on. "I think I gasped, because he turned around and looked at me. His face was… I can't describe it. He was surprised, and angry, but then angry because he was surprised, as well.

"It was like we were all frozen for a minute, and then he backed away from my mum and came up to me. Mum tried to say something to him. I don't know what, and he didn't listen. He got in my face and I flinched. I expected him to yell, or hit me, but he told me to get out, his voice low and serious. I looked at my mum, wondering if I was ever gonna see her again, because I thought he meant I had to leave, like Zhara. Find somewhere else to live.

"Mum opened her mouth to say something else—it was bleeding. Her lip. I remember blood—but before she got the words out Kian screamed "now!" and I jumped. It was so loud, and he was right beside me. It sounded like a cannon going off or something.

"I ran out into the back garden but didn't know what to do—what he wanted me to do. When he kicked Zhara out, he let her pack a bag. But it wasn't like I was gonna go back inside to try that. So, I just stood there. It was so cold, but I didn't want to walk back to school. What would I have told my teachers? I didn't think they'd believe me. A-and I didn't really understand what had happened."

"How long did you stand outside?" asked Mitch, when Mya went silent for a while.

She clenched her fists. "It was hours. I know it was—actual, literal hours—because it started to get dark. When the adrenaline wore off, I really needed the toilet, but I was still too scared to move. I…" Mya had never told anyone any of this, and her mum never talked about it afterwards, but despite the embarrassment of the next bit in particular, somehow she got the words out.

"My feet went numb, and I couldn't hop around. You know how you do when you need the toilet, but can't go? I…" She bit her lip. "I wet myself. Like I was five again. The pee trickled down my legs and into my socks, where it froze.

"Eventually, my mum came out and found me. She brought me in and gave me a long bath, warming the water up slowly. Kian had gone somewhere. Or, at least, I didn't see him. He may have been drinking in their room or something. Things got a little blurry, at that point.

"I ended up really sick. Stuck in bed with a fever, and a cough. It was bad enough, Kian actually let Mum get a doctor to come out to the house. I don't know what she told him, but he said I needed 'extended bedrest.' When school started back, I didn't go. I missed most of the next term, and then I was too far behind, so…"

Mya swallowed and looked up again. "They kept me back a year."

Mitch's eyes were heavy with something. Mya could tell he was biting his tongue. She actually thought he might want to cry along with her, but eventually he just said, "Thank you for sharing that. That was… well." He forced a smile. "We picked quite the place to start off, didn't we?"

"It's okay," Mya lied, looking at the clock again. They'd gone over their slot by five minutes. "I'm sorry I went on so long."

"Sometimes, we need to," said Mitch. "Same time next week?"

She nodded and got up to lift Emma. Jane picked them up again, taking them home. Mya got the impression that Jane wanted to ask how the session went, but she held herself back and Mya didn't volunteer the information. It would be too much like going over it all again.

Just like after the first session, Mya felt exhausted. Like she'd been hit by a train. Somehow, she made it through the motions of feeding Emma and changing her nappy. Mya even managed to remember to change her own clothes for bed, but she forgot to lock her door—something she only became aware of when it opened in the middle of the night, and someone tried to come in.

Mya sat up and stared blearily at them, half-blinded by the light in the hall. She was so out of it, it didn't even register that she should be scared. She just looked at the person who'd come halfway into her room, uninvited, while she slept, and tried to process what was happening.

Eventually, her brain at least registered who the person was.

Katie.

Chapter Fourteen

"Katie?"

She jumped at the sound of her name and ran back into the hall, Mya's bedroom door slamming behind her. Then Emma woke up and started screaming. *Shit.* No matter that Mya's heart had started hammering in her chest, she was still half asleep and couldn't quite get her legs to work properly as she made her way across the room to her daughter.

Mya stumbled, bashing her hip into the edge of the chest of drawers, and had to clamp her jaw shut to stop herself from swearing again out loud. Shuffling the rest of the short distance to Emma, she picked her up and rocked her a little.

Mya made as many soothing sounds as she could muster, but it quickly became clear that Emma wasn't going to settle again anytime soon. *Suppose I might as well deal with issue number two*, thought Mya. She briefly made sure her nightdress was straight—not riding up to expose anything she wanted to keep hidden—then hiked Emma higher in her arms, and went out into the hall.

It was empty, all doors closed except the one that led to the kitchen, which was in darkness. Mya kept rocking Emma as she walked down to Katie's door and knocked.

There was no response at first, but then Mya heard footsteps. She braced herself for… something. A fight? A conversation? At this point, Mya had no idea what reaction or explanation she was likely to be presented with, but had just thought that nothing would surprise her when Bernice opened her door and the sound of her own screaming child followed her out.

"If you don't mind, some of us are trying to sleep!"

"I'm sorry," said Mya. "Emma will calm down soon. We didn't mean to wake you."

Bernice wrapped her nightgown more firmly around herself and crossed her arms. She looked more closely at Emma. "Well, what's wrong with her? And why are you out in the hallway? You'll catch your death of cold in that nightdress. I'm not surprised Emma's screaming if you're–"

"Oh, for God's sake!" Mya couldn't help but roll her eyes. It was only when Bernice visibly looked taken aback that she realised she'd exclaimed out loud.

"I really would have expected better of you, Mya."

Mya could tell she was about to launch into a lecture, and she couldn't take it. She'd been unceremoniously ripped from the first solid sleep she'd had since she'd given birth, had her private space invaded, and had two screaming babies to listen to.

"Just piss off, Bernice. Why don't you sort out your own kid, mind your own business and leave me alone, yeah?"

Bernice's face fell. Mya could practically see all of her words instantly vanishing, which she considered no mean feat, and guilt stabbed at her. But in the next instant, Bernice's expression twisted into a mime of a bulldog chewing a wasp and she snapped right back.

"*You* piss off, Mya. You, and Lynne, and the lot of you. I won't miss any of you when I move out on Monday!" Her voice caught on the word 'Monday' and Mya thought she saw tears in the corners of her eyes, but before she could get a really good look, Bernice had slammed her door—something which made both Emma and Bernice's own child cry louder.

Mya had no idea how Lynne hadn't woken up and wasn't also giving her an earful, and she had no idea what to think about Bernice's comment about moving out—it was certainly the first she'd heard of it—but she didn't have a lot of brain power to process it, right that second.

"Shh, now," she told Emma softly. "Come on, it's okay." Mya kept rocking her in one arm and knocked on Katie's door again with her free hand, determined to get to the bottom of things so that she could go back to sleep and finally put the whole awful, weird experience behind her.

"Katie, let me in right now," she said through the door, half-whispering so as not to annoy Bernice again, but trying to sound strong at the same time, so Katie would take her seriously.

Nothing happened.

"Katie," Mya tried again. "If you don't let me in, I'm going to call the police."

There was the sound of footsteps again, and Mya bit her lip, but they sounded both quieter and closer than Bernice's had been. After a moment, Katie opened her door and Mya stepped inside.

***

Katie's room was not at all like Mya had expected it. She may not have actually given it that much thought, but considering that Katie was always so quiet and kept to herself, if Mya had thought about it, she would have expected minimalism: clean surfaces with everything in its place. What she saw instead was an assortment of toys and clothes everywhere, an overflowing wastepaper bin, and posters covering every available square inch of wall.

Mya walked in a slow circle, trying to take it in, and saw the posters were on the back of the door and on the ceiling, too. It made the already small room feel claustrophobic, and Mya even more confused about her flatmate.

Katie was standing in the middle of the room, her arms wrapped around herself in a defensive way, just staring at her bare feet. She mumbled something Mya didn't catch, and Mya had to ask her to repeat it.

There was a pause, then, "Please don't call the police," Katie whispered.

Mya opened her mouth to ask what the hell she thought she was doing, but then she looked past Katie to where Sarah was standing up in her cot, looking utterly bewildered. Mya wiped a hand down her face and took a deep breath, hoping that Emma would just stop crying so she could think straight.

"Listen," Mya told Katie. "I'm going to try and feed her. Can we sit down and talk?"

Katie glanced nervously at the door, then at Mya, but eventually nodded. It wasn't like she had much choice.

"Right," said Mya. She sat on the edge of Katie's bed and pulled up her nightdress to uncover her left breast. It was awkward as all hell, because she of course only had a regular nightdress, not one of those special ones with flaps that at least helped a little with modesty, but Emma latched on and started to suckle.

Mya felt herself sag in the relief of her silence. "So," she said to Katie after a minute, "why were you in my room?"

Katie shook her head. "N-no. I… I wasn't… it–I didn't…"

"Stop," said Mya. Katie was still standing in the middle of the room and looked ready to bolt. Mya wasn't having it. She was way too tired for this shit. "Where are you gonna run to? You can't leave Sarah."

Katie's eyes flicked to her daughter, she swallowed, and then sat.

"Okay," said Mya, taking a deep breath. She wanted to shake Katie, or at least yell at her, but figured that wouldn't help a damn thing. "There's no point trying to deny you were in my room, because I saw you. Let's go back to the start. The first night I moved in here, did you go through my bag?"

Katie wrung her hands, and it was the first time Mya noticed that she had big angry welts on the skin there, like she'd washed them in boiling water.

"Is it you that keeps setting off the fire alarms?" Mya pressed.

Katie shook her head again—more violently than before—and began another string of denials.

Mya held up a hand. She couldn't exactly explain why, and didn't think her now pounding head could bear any more stammering, but her gut said Katie wasn't lying. "You didn't set off the alarms. But you did go through my bag, is that right?"

"I d-didn't," said Katie, and Mya groaned, ready to storm out and follow through on her threat to call the police, because that part was obviously B.S., but then Katie said, "– mean to. D-didn't mean to. Can't." She shook her head so hard, it looked in danger of falling off her neck, and tears had started to form in the corners of her eyes. "I can't help it."

"Breathe," said Mya, partly because crying was only going to make getting details out of Katie harder, but also because she'd already upset Bernice, and if Katie was also gonna be upset, Mya felt she might as well go piss off Lynne for good measure, too. Go all in, three for three.

They sat in silence for a while as Mya tried to figure out exactly how to proceed.

Sarah started babbling and Katie went over to her, lifting her out of her cot and bringing her over to the bed, where she cradled her on her lap. Mya watched as Katie practically transformed in front of her eyes. Holding Sarah was like a magical act, because as soon as she had her settled, Katie herself looked a thousand times more comfortable.

"I'm sorry," she said at last, her voice no longer shaking.

Mya stared at her, still trying to make sense of it. "What happened?"

Katie closed her eyes and pressed her face close to Sarah's scalp, like she was breathing her in. Mya didn't think she was going to answer her again, but finally she said, "I don't know if... if I can explain. I'm not quite myself."

"When?" asked Mya.

"When they come."

God, it was like pulling teeth. "They?"

"I get thoughts," said Katie, only to shake her head again. The movement was less frantic now. "No. They're more than thoughts. I think they called it compulsions."

"Who called it that?" asked Mya.

Katie waved a hand. "The internet. A website. I typed in my symptoms, and..." She shrugged.

Mya blinked at her. "So... you get compulsions that take you over?" Somehow, this wasn't making her feel any better. "Compulsions to steal things?"

Katie opened her eyes and pinned Mya with a look of utter offense. "No! I don't steal. I..." Sarah flinched in her arms and she lowered her voice. "I *check* things."

Mya rubbed her temple and moved Emma over to her other breast. *Just let this be over so I can go back to sleep, please!* "You check things? What does that even mean? What kind of things?"

"I told you," said Katie. "I can't explain. Don't understand it myself."

Mya sighed. "Well, how long have you had compulsions?" *I will get to the bottom of this, I swear to god.*

Katie didn't answer, but focused her eyes on the back of Sarah's head, and that seemed like answer enough. For them to have ended up in a Mother and Baby Unit, Mya figured that some kind of tragedy or trauma must have befallen them, but it wasn't her business to pry. She needed to know she was safe living in the flat and nothing more.

"How often do you feel like this?" Mya asked, changing tack, and Katie shrugged.

"It's different. Different times. I've never found a pattern to it."

Mya had to swallow another groan, because she still had very little idea of what they were actually talking about.

"It's not easy, you know!" said Katie sharply, taking Mya aback.

"Fine. It's not easy," said Mya. "I don't even care, but you can see why I'm asking. I mean, you have to see why I'm so freaked!"

Katie deflated again. "Mostly it's when things change," she admitted, in lieu of continuing down the path of an argument. "New place. New people. Can be anything."

Okay. So that kind of tracked with Mya moving in. "But why tonight? Nothing changed tonight."

"You had a boy," said Katie.

"Eh?" Mya had to rearrange Emma a little, but she was so frustrated with the conversation, she barely cared about the fact that she was practically flashing her flatmate anymore. "Emma's a girl. I had a girl. And this isn't new."

"No," said Katie. "Before. Outside. I saw you."

Mya wracked her brain trying to think of whatever Katie was talking about, but eventually something clicked. She'd had a boy. A visitor. Richard.

"You mean when someone came to talk to me the other day?"

Katie nodded. "I saw him and I had to check. Tonight was the first chance I got. You didn't lock your door."

I won't be making that mistake again in a hurry, Mya thought but didn't say. "You know you can't just do that," she told Katie instead. "It's creepy. And illegal."

Katie at least had the good grace to look shamed. "I'm sorry," she told Mya. "I am. I know it's wrong, but I can't help it."

Mya pushed her admonishment aside, because all it had done was bring them back to the start of the conversation. Emma was growing restless, and Mya didn't want to regress even further, to being entirely confused and having a child screaming in her ear. *Better find a way to wrap this up.*

"Listen," she said, "I don't really get what you're supposed to be checking for, or why, but I'm willing to believe that you're not a bad person. I…" Mya paused, because this is where things could really fall down. "I think you need help, Katie. I think you need help, and Patsy should probably be able to point you in the right direction. Or your doctor. If they don't help, we can try another Google search. The NHS website, or something. But you've got to find a way to stop this, do you understand?"

Katie had closed her eyes again, but she took a deep breath. "I do. I understand."

"Because, you know if you don't get help, it's going to keep happening and you'll end up in more trouble," Mya continued. "If you walk into someone else's room like you did to mine, they might not be so understanding."

"I know," said Katie. "You're right. I know you are. It's just…"

"Hard?" said Mya. "Yeah, you said. But you've got this. You have to. You…" She looked at Sarah, starting to nod off right there in Katie's lap. "You've got Sarah. Why don't you try and do it for her?"

Katie sniffled but didn't seem able to say much else, so Mya finished up feeding Emma and told her goodnight. She trudged back to her room, wondering if she should knock on Bernice's door as she passed it and try to apologise, but figured it would be best left to morning. As she locked her door and got settled back into bed for the night, Mya thought that if her flatmate really was moving out, they should probably do something for her.

Though what, she had no idea.

Chapter Fifteen

"We're going to throw her an *Ann Summers* party."

Mya stared at Lynne, her spoon paused halfway to her mouth. "You're going to what?"

"We," said Lynne, "not just me. It'll be fun."

"I'm under eighteen," Mya reminded her. "And none of us have any money."

Lynne winked. "We don't have to tell the rep that."

Mya laughed, but Lynne seemed entirely serious. Or maybe *because* she was serious. It couldn't actually work, could it? "Bernice doesn't strike me as an *Ann Summers* kind of person. And isn't it too short notice? She's leaving on Monday."

"All in hand, duck. I've already made the call and got someone lined up for the evening."

"The evening? As in, *this* evening? Today?" Lynne grinned and Mya couldn't help but laugh again. "You're unbelievable!"

"I know," said Lynne. "Now, come and help me with this."

She'd made a banner out of some toilet roll and black felt tip pen, and gotten a packet of balloons from the pound shop.

Mya set her cereal aside and stood up to grab her half of the balloons, ready to get blowing. "When did you even hear she was moving out?"

"Yesterday, when you were w' your quack."

Mya resented Mitch being called a quack, but it felt like too much energy to try and fight the point, so she let it slide. "Where is she moving to?"

"Council finally found her a flat, I think."

Lynne tried to lift the sofa and move it backwards, to make more room for... a demonstration from the rep later? Mya seriously hoped not, it was super cringe just thinking about it. She nudged Lynne out of the way and took over.

"You're way too pregnant to be moving things."

"Fine," said Lynne. "I'm due a fag break anyway."

"Don't let Bernice catch you, you know she's just dying to tell you again that–"

Lynne cleared her throat and Mya looked up from the sofa to see Bernice had materialised in the doorway. Lynne moved past her and pulled a face Mya interpreted as, 'well, you're in the shit now. Thank god I was already on my way out.'

"Uh, hi" Mya shifted the sofa the last couple of inches and stepped back. "You want a seat?"

Bernice pursed her lips and went over to her cupboard, deftly ignoring the offer.

Mya sighed. "Listen, Bernie–" Bernice gave her a sharp look and Mya cringed. "Bernice, sorry. I wanted to apologise."

She stopped rearranging her pair of tea mugs and turned around, crossing her arms. "I'm listening."

Mya's mouth went dry. "I, um… last night. I…"

"You yelled at me," said Bernice. "After *you* woke *me* up."

"Right. That."

"If you'd yelled at me after I woke you up, I could understand it," Bernice continued, "but no. I got to play both victim and villain. How do you think that makes me feel?"

Mya just about resisted the urge to roll her eyes. She opened her mouth to issue the standard 'sorry' again instead, but Bernice cut her off.

"I know what you all think of me," she went on. "I know you laugh at me, and like to call me names. But I do have feelings, you know?"

Crap. It looked like she was going to cry again. And she did have a point. Mya knew she could be hot-headed, sometimes, but she'd never considered herself a bully. The thought was repulsive—because it would put her on a par with Kian, wouldn't it?—but the truth was that she hadn't treated her flatmate very well. Annoying or not, Bernice didn't deserve to be left in tears.

"I do know that," said Mya, actively infusing the words with as much sincerity as she could muster. "I was wrong to yell, and I'm sorry I woke you up. And for the teasing. I promise it stops now. Will you let me make it up to you?"

Bernice wavered for a minute, as if unsure if she was going to give into her tears, or push past them. "Make it up how?"

Mya reached behind Bernice, into the still open cupboard, and picked up her favourite mug. "How about we start with a cup of tea?"

"Well, all right," said Bernice, sniffing. She walked over to the sofa and sat down. "But use the good tea bags."

We have good tea bags? Mya raised an eyebrow, surprised and a little impressed that Bernice had been holding out on her. Yes, they had their own cupboards, but they typically shared the essentials, and tea was definitely considered one of those.

Mya followed Bernice's gaze back to her cupboard, and moved things around to find a packet of Tetley hidden away at the back. *Huh.*

"You can have one, too," said Bernice, amicably.

"Uh, thanks," replied Mya, lifting the kettle. She'd kind of figured that went without saying, but nothing ever went without saying with Bernice.

Bernice lifted the toilet roll off the floor between her finger and thumb. "So, what's all this, then?"

"Didn't Lynne tell you?"

Bernice narrowed her eyes. "Tell me what?"

Please, please don't hate this idea. "We're throwing you a party. That's your banner."

"Oh!"

Mya bit her lip, waiting for Bernice to stomp off, offended, or maybe start a rant, but her expression softened. She smiled sadly at the banner and set it down carefully beside her.

"I've never had a party before."

Mya blinked at her. "Never?" Even she'd had parties as a child, before Kian came along.

Bernice sighed wistfully and picked up a balloon, lifting the foul-smelling cheap rubber to her nose and inhaling with a smile. "I suppose there's a first time for everything."

"Yeah," said Mya, though what she really supposed––or maybe hoped—was that it meant Bernice would have low expectations, and not be too disappointed when her party turned out to be an opportunity to examine sex toys.

***

Nicole the *Ann Summers* representative showed up at 8:15, weighed down with an assortment of bags and boxes, and a clipboard. Lynne had gone all out, buying a giant bag of Tesco value cheese puffs for everyone to share, and Katie had even prised herself from her room to watch the festivities unfold.

Mya helped Nicole set up, finding her places to set her items so they wouldn't fall down, but were still in easy reach, and waited. She caught the exact moment Nicole looked up long enough to notice the small crowd included a toddler and two babies.

Her mouth hung open a little bit.

"Drink?" asked Mya. "We have water and, uh…" She didn't know if she was allowed to offer Bernice's good tea, and felt a little embarrassed to offer the terrible stuff. "Water?"

"Oh, give her a real drink," said Lynne, reaching into the carrier bag at her feet for a four-pack of cider and handing one to Nicole.

Mya felt her eyes almost bug out of her head. "Lynne, you can't–"

"Hush," said Bernice, reaching for the second can and cracking it open. "It's a party."

Lynne laughed and opened her own can, clicking it with Bernice's. "Cheers!"

Katie got the fourth can, and Mya was granted permission to keep using the good tea bags.

"What is this place?" asked Nicole. "I assumed it was some kind of student apartment, but–" She gestured to Emma and Sarah.

"We're runaways," said Lynne.

Bernice cackled. "Kidnappers!"

"Oh, that's a good one," said Lynne, grinning.

Mya shook her head and told Nicole, "We're harmless. And lightweights, apparently."

"Boo!" said Lynne. "Now shut up and let the girl get started. I want to see the really big ones first."

Bernice and Katie giggled and Mya stared at each of them, then looked back at Nicole, who seemed just as bemused as she felt.

"I brought a… Oh, where is it?" She shuffled around in her boxes, then slapped a hand to her forehead. "I think I've left it on the bus."

The peanut gallery laughed harder and Nicole cringed.

"It's okay," said Mya, though she was trying hard not to laugh herself now. The earlier conversation with Bernice was still playing on Mya's mind, so she was trying to be extra nice. *Don't want to upset anyone else.* "We can maybe call the bus company and–"

Nicole was shaking her head. "This is a disaster. I've been here ten minutes and already broken three of the rules."

Mya forced a smile. "We won't tell anyone."

"'Course we won't!" echoed Lynne and Bernice.

"They are having the time of their lives," said Mya. "That's because of you. Don't feel too bad."

Nicole cracked a tiny smile. "I think it's because of the cider. But, um…" She bit her lip and leaned close to Mya's ear. "Tell me honestly, were any of you likely to buy anything anyway?"

Mya felt the smile on her face turn guilty and Nicole sighed in response. "Oh, well. I only took the stupid gig to make my mum happy."

"Your mum wanted you to go around trying to sell sex toys?" Mya questioned, dubious. *Now this sounds interesting.*

"Well." Nicole blushed. "She told me to get a job. It was my bright idea to pick the most ridiculous one I could find to shame her back into paying my tuition fees. Just wait until she hears about this."

"Good on you, girl!" Lynne yelled, even though she was right there.

Bernice told her to 'shh.'

"Oh, shh yourself!"

Bernice scoffed. "Excuse me!"

Mya and Katie exchanged a look at their bickering, then Mya turned back to Nicole. "Sorry we wasted your time. You should stay and at least finish your drink."

Nicole considered it for a moment, then said, "What the hell," and necked it. "It's not like I'm driving. Let's just hope I don't end up with the same bus driver home." She did an impersonation of a stuffy old man. "*Excuse me, Miss, is this your dildo?*"

Mya couldn't help it, she joined in the cackling and sat back to listen to Nicole recount horror stories her fellow reps told her. "I've only been in the job one week, and already had some idiot guys book me for just a laugh, a teenager accidentally flash me when her mum didn't warn her in advance that she had guests in the living room, and a dog chase me down the street."

Katie shook her head, but was smiling to herself. "I'm going to bed," she announced, setting her can down and lifting Sarah.

Lynne looked so baffled by hearing her speak, she didn't say anything about the criminally early night, and Bernice lifted the can and pressed it to her lips.

"What?" she said, when everyone stared at her. "She barely touched it!"

Next to bed was Emma, who Mya quickly fed and bathed before going back into the living area. Nicole had apparently left in her absence, and Bernice was three sheets to the wind, singing tunelessly to herself.

"You only had a can and a half," said Lynne, incredulous.

"You're one to talk," said Mya. "You haven't even finished your can and you're swaying."

"I am not!" she protested, punctuating it with a hiccup. "And anyway, it's not me. It's the baby."

"Uh huh," said Mya. "I'm pretty sure babies aren't supposed to drink."

"Only one," said Bernice, who pulled herself upright suddenly, holding a hand to her head. "I think I need to lie down—on something that isn't spinning."

Mya frowned and offered her a hand up from the sofa, but Bernice waved it away. "I can do it!" It took her twenty minutes and three attempts, but she did in fact make it back into her own room.

"Looks like it's just you and me, duck," said Lynne. She started wriggling around.

"What are you doing?"

"Trying to figure out which pocket me phone's in. Here!" She pulled it out and passed it to Mya.

"What do you want me to do with it?"

"Music!" Lynne yelled.

"Shh!" said Mya. "Everyone's gone to bed, and probably gonna be hungover soon enough."

"Music!" Lynne yelled again.

Mya rolled her eyes and started scrolling through her files, thinking that if she played something quietly in the background, it would be better than Lynne continuously making noise.

"Lynne, you've only got, like, three songs."

"So?"

"Two of them are *Wonderwall* and one of them is something I can't even pronounce!"

"So?" Lynne repeated, hiccupping again.

Mya shook her head. "I think, maybe, it's time you went to bed."

"No," said Lynne, "I want music. Come on, Mya. You can sing along. You know the words, right?"

"Mya's tired," said Mya. "I need to put you to bed and have some peace and quiet."

"Spoil-sport!" said Lynne in a sing-songy voice.

Mya sighed, exasperated, but she couldn't resist the smile tugging at her lips. "Don't you want me to tuck you in? I could read you a story."

"Music!" demanded Lynne.

Good grief, she was worse than Emma when she didn't want her nap.

"I'll sing *Twinkle Twinkle Little Star* if you just stand up," said Mya in a last-ditch effort. It didn't feel right to leave Lynne on her own out in the living area. God only knew what would happen if she lit up inside, or tried to cook something once the post-alcohol munchies kicked in.

"Here." Mya got her half hauled up by her arm, but Lynne wriggled at the last moment and they lost balance, Lynne falling to the floor squarely on her tailbone.

"Oh, god! Are you okay?"

Lynne laughed. "Stop fussing. I'm–" She giggled some more, but sounded a little winded. "–fine."

When Mya tried to help her up again, she at least didn't try struggling again. Mya thought she'd finally won and imagined being all curled up in bed in just a few short minutes, but then she noticed a dark patch on the carpet. It only took her a moment to figure out what it was.

"Oh, my god!"

Lynne laughed and continued pulling on Mya's arm.

"Lynne, stop. You need to sit down."

"Ha! I thought you were taking me to bed."

"Lynne, I'm serious. Your waters broke!"

134

Chapter Sixteen

"Lynne, your waters broke!" Mya said it twice, and still Lynne didn't seem to be getting it.

"Oh, they're fine," she said, waving Mya away.

"No, Lynne, listen to me. You're having your baby." Lynne stared at her, and "Now!" Mya had to add for emphasis. She could tell the instant Lynne was sober again, because she started crying.

"Oh, no. Come on, now. It's okay," Mya soothed.

"'S'not," Lynne hiccuped. "I'm not ready." She took Mya's hand in a death grip, staring right in her eyes. "This can't happen. Mya, you can't let it happen!"

"Take it easy," said Mya, still trying to keep her words calm, despite the fact that she could feel herself starting to freak out—palms sweating and heart thumping. "Just breathe. I'm right here, and you'll get through this."

Lynne shook her head. "I can't. I– I'm not–" She couldn't finish for sobbing so hard.

Mya didn't know if it was the right thing, but went with her instinct to hug Lynne, cradling her head to her chest until she got past the worst of it and at least seemed able to breathe again. Mya figured they'd have lots of time to gather themselves and get sorted, given how long labour usually took, but this one was already so unlike Mya's. By the time Mya's waters had broken, she'd been having contractions for hours, whereas this seemed to be spontaneous. Though it struck Mya that she should check, just to be sure.

"Hey, Lynne?"

Lynne looked up at her, tears tracked down her cheeks and expression pitiful. It made her seem so much younger than she was.

"Lynne, are you in any pain?"

She held a hand to her back. "Got a twinge."

"Okay, and what else?" asked Mya, a tick list forming in her mind. *I should check something. Maybe everything. What should I check first?* "Have you had any other pain today? Before you fell?"

Lynne shook her head and Mya bit her lip. *Maybe I'm jumping the gun. Maybe she wet herself. God, I'm so out of my depth!*

Mya so wanted to get an adult to take over, only belatedly realising that she herself qualified as one. Even so, she told Lynne to "stay put" and tried knocking on Katie and Bernice's doors.

Neither answered.

Lack of response from Bernice, Mya could understand. She'd seemed really far gone on the cider. And Katie was probably being Katie, not coming out of her room or responding to anyone except on her own terms, or where needed. Mya reckoned she could probably convince her, but didn't think it was worth wasting the time. She didn't strike Mya as the best in stressful situations.

Fuck. I may be almost an adult, but this needs someone else. Who else is there?

Mya went into her room and came back out with her phone and the bit of paper she'd been given when she first arrived, with Patsy's number on it. *'For use in case of emergencies.'*

Mya dialled, but there was no answer. She tried twice more as she paced up and down the hall, and then phoned Jane, who had her 'out of office' setting turned on, directing everything to voicemail.

That left one option. Mya took a deep breath and dialled 999.

"Which service do you need?"

"Ambulance. My friend is–"

"One moment." There was a clicking sound, a pause, then another voice.

"Ambulance service. You're speaking to Olivia. Can I take your name?"

Mya went back into the kitchen-cum-living-area and put her hand on Lynne's shoulder. "My friend's in labour. I mean, I think she is. She's–"

"Your name?" Olivia asked again.

"Mya," said Mya, "but that's not important. My friend needs–"

"Okay, Mya, what's your friend's name?"

"Lynne."

Lynne mumbled something at the same time the dispatcher asked her next question, and Mya had to tell Olivia to hang on.

"What was that, Lynne?"

"Lynnette Kirk. It's me full name. They'll need it."

"Right." Mya turned her attention back to her phone, the 'low battery' warning of which was flashing. *Because that's exactly what I bloody well need.*

"I'm going to need some more details," Olivia was saying. "Can I have Lynne's full name, and your address?"

Mya told her both, then had to repeat the issue.

"What do you mean when you say you *think* she's in labour?" asked Olivia.

Mya rubbed her forehead, just wishing she'd send someone already. "Lynne's pregnant. Heavily pregnant. Almost due. She fell, and there's a stain. I think her waters broke."

"All right," said Olivia. "Someone's on their way now. Are you able to stand outside and make sure they're able to get in all right?"

"I'm not leaving Lynne."

"Is there anyone else with you?"

"No."

"All right," Olivia said again. "I can tell you when they're close. In the meantime–"

Lynne groaned, and Mya tuned out the rest of what Olivia was saying.

"What's wrong? You okay?"

"Hurts," said Lynne.

"Mya? Mya, are you still there?" Olivia was asking.

"I'm still here. Lynne says she hurts. I think maybe contractions are starting. I don't know."

"The ambulance is three minutes away," said Olivia. "Will the paramedics be able to access the building?"

Mya's mind spun as Lynne started panting. She couldn't think or say anything for a moment, then, "Gate," she managed. "There's a gate."

"Mya, I need you to go outside and open the gate for the paramedics."

"But–"

"They can't help your friend if they can't get to her," Olivia said reasonably.

"O-okay. Yeah, I…" Mya looked from Lynne, who was clutching her hand again, to the door. "Yeah, I can do that. How close are they now?"

"Two minutes. I need you to go outside now. It'll help them to know they've got the right place."

"Right." Mya explained this to Lynne, who had started crying again. She didn't seem willing to let go of Mya's hand.

"One minute away," said Olivia. "Are you outside now?"

Mya took a deep breath and all but had to prise herself out of Lynne's grip. She ran out of the living area into the hall, and was about to go from there into the other hall that had the staircase to the upstairs flat and door to the courtyard when she realised she had to make a brief detour into her room for her keys, otherwise they wouldn't be able to get back in.

"Almost there!" Mya told Olivia. She was out of breath and trying to ignore Lynne wailing in the background. When Mya went back in her room, Emma started to stir in response to the disruption, and Mya was pretty sure she was gonna join in crying soon enough, but she couldn't focus on that for the moment either.

Mya got outside and jogged across the courtyard in bare feet, reaching the gate at the same time as the paramedics appeared on the other side. She let them in—a black man and white woman–and led them to Lynne in a blur.

As they knelt down, putting on gloves and whipping out a blood pressure cuff, Mya shrank back. She could feel her thoughts retreating and eyes glazing over, as if her brain had overwhelmed itself and going into 'read only' mode, but then Emma did indeed start crying and everything jolted back into place. Mya walked down the hall and into her room, picking Emma up and hugging her tight.

Emma calmed a little and Mya carried her back out into the hall, over to the kitchen door. From there, Mya watched as the paramedics helped Lynne to her feet, balancing her weight between them. One of them—the woman—was explaining that she was going to walk with Lynne out to the door, where the man would have a stretcher waiting.

The man went out past Mya, presumably to get it set up, and Lynne looked up, catching Mya's eye.

"I'm in a right state, ain't I?" She forced a smile, but it twisted into a grimace at the last moment.

"You're getting there." the paramedic told her, pausing until the contraction passed before guiding Lynne the rest of the way into the hall.

"Are you coming with us?" the paramedic asked Mya.

"Of course," said Mya, only to pause. "I need to get Emma some things."

"I don't think baby is for waiting," said the paramedic, not unkindly. "You know you can't take her with you." She nodded at Emma.

"But she's– I mean–" Mya stammered, only to be cut off by Lynne groaning again.

"Mya," she said through gritted teeth. "Please."

"Lynne, I–"

The paramedic kept moving her down the hall, clearly serious about the not waiting thing. "If you've got no one to leave her with, we'll head on."

Mya followed her out into the courtyard, Emma still in her arms, at a loss for what to do. Lynne was begging Mya not to leave her, but she couldn't very well abandon Emma. Lynne had to understand that.

Lynne evidently didn't understand much. She started struggling against the paramedics as they put her on the stretcher. They shared a look, then began strapping Lynne down, so she didn't fall off.

"Mya!" Lynne screamed as she was wheeled away, back through the gate and into the back of the ambulance. "Mya, you bitch, I won't forgive you for this!"

Mya could only stare after her, her heart shuddering as the paramedics shut the doors and set off, siren wailing. Mya's phone buzzed to let her know it was powering down due to the low battery, and only then did she realise she never properly ended the call with Olivia.

Shit, I screwed this whole thing up. But Lynne will be okay. She has to be okay.

"What's going on?"

Mya jumped at the question and turned to see Patsy had appeared from somewhere. Her room, Mya supposed. But if she was there the whole time, why hadn't she answered her phone, and how had she not heard all of the noise before the siren started up? Had she just not cared?

"Mya?" Patsy questioned, eyeing the gate that the paramedic left open.

"Lynne," said Mya. "Labour." She couldn't seem to form any other words—or none that were swear-free, because damn, she was pissed. It should have been Patsy dealing with the paramedics, and Lynne, and all of it.

How come I got help and I'm the one Lynne doesn't forgive? Mya had a pretty good idea that Lynne hadn't known what she was saying, or didn't mean it even if she had, but it still stung. Probably more than it should have, and definitely more than if someone had said it to Mya before all the Emma stuff. Back when she had more than one real friend, and could talk things out with the others if one of them fell out with her for some reason. Find some kind of comfort.

Patsy was asking something else, but Mya wasn't listening. If Patsy didn't have the details, it was her own fault. *Hers, not mine.*

"I'm going to bed," said Mya, turning on her heel and going directly to her room even as Patsy called after her.

Mya got Emma resettled, plugged her phone in, and sat down on the bed, pulling the duvet around her.

What now? Despite the tiredness eating at her from the inside, Mya didn't hold out much hope for sleep. At least not for a while. Her brain kept replaying Lynne being strapped down, screaming at her; her whole face scarlet with pain and rage.

Mya's phone jingled as it came back to life, causing her to flinch. Mya shook her head. *I should be better than this. Shouldn't be jumping at every little thing—or taking shit for doing my best.*

In a flash of inspiration, Mya lifted her phone and jabbed it until she was calling Zhara.

"Hey."

"Don't hey me!"

"Mya?"

"Who'd you think?"

"Mya?" Zhara questioned again. "Why are you yelling at me? What's wrong?"

"Me, apparently. That's what everyone thinks!"

"Mya, what the hell are you talking about?"

Mya groaned and followed it up with a deep breath, but didn't answer.

"Are you safe?" Zhara asked.

"Yes," said Mya, mollified a little by the concern.

"Okay. So…"

Mya sighed. "I called to yell at you. That was it."

"Why?" asked Zhara, which made Mya sit up with surprise so fast, she almost pulled her phone accidentally out from the wall.

"You don't know why I'm mad? Didn't you listen? Or remember our last conversation?"

Zhara paused, and for a brief moment Mya worried that her sister's thing about suppressing bad memories didn't just apply to their childhood.

"This is about dad?" Zhara asked at last, at least putting to bed that theory.

Mya sighed again and rubbed at her temples. "It's about me being sick of being blamed for shit. I'm not gonna just take it anymore."

Zhara paused again, then said, "All right, I shouldn't have sworn at you. I just don't get how you can forgive Dad."

"Hang on," said Mya. "Who said I forgave him?"

"You went to see him, didn't you?"

"That's not the same thing, Zhara."

Zhara sighed down the phone. "Fine, whatever. It's done. I promise not to yell at you again, are you happy?"

Mya grunted and could almost hear Zhara roll her eyes in response.

"I'm going back to sleep, okay?"

"Wait," said Mya.

"What am I waiting for?"

Mya hesitated, then, "I love you, Zhara. I know I don't tell you enough, but–"

"I love you, too."

Mya's mouth split into a smile so wide, it made her cheeks hurt, and her eyes started to mist over. "You love me even when we fight?"

"Especially when we fight."

Mya laughed. "That doesn't even make sense."

"So?" Zhara challenged, and Mya shook her head.

"Goodnight, Zhara."

"You sure you're okay?"

"So long as we are," said Mya.

"We're cool," said Zhara. "Night."

Mya hugged the phone to her chest when the call disconnected, reassured that she wasn't just some loner that alienated everyone. She even decided to text Richard the next day, to see if he might like to spend a little more time with Emma.

That settled in her mind, Mya set the phone down to finish charging and curled in a ball, ready to put the day behind her.

Chapter Seventeen

Sunday was a day of sleeping in and ultra-cheap hangover cures, which was basically tap water and the leftover cheese puffs. Mya helped Bernice pack her meager possessions and did her best to keep her glass topped up, gritting her teeth through all of her flatmate's moaning and groaning.

By the time Monday morning rolled around, things were set. Bernice was ready to go, and Mya had settled some things in her mind. No more sitting around waiting for things to be fixed, hoping they'd work out on their own. She'd texted Richard as planned, and he'd agreed to mind Emma for a few hours, which left Mya free to visit Lynne in hospital. If the visit went well and Mya wasn't left feeling crushed, she had plans to try and get through to her aunt again, having written out what she planned to say in advance this time. Before that, though…

"Katie?" Mya knocked twice on her door, and she eventually opened it. "Hey. I just wanted to check how you were."

Katie shrugged—the action more uncomfortable than casual—and didn't move aside, silently welcoming Mya into her room the way Lynne would have.

"Listen," Mya continued, undeterred, "I know what you said about change being a trigger or whatever. With Bernice leaving and Lynne in hospital, coming back with her kid in a couple of days, I wanted to… you know."

Katie looked away, which left Mya feeling super awkward. *How many ways can I phrase 'I'm checking up on you' before it comes across as more of a threat than someone actually trying to make sure you're fine?*

"Have you spoken to Patsy yet?"

"Today," said Katie, wringing her hands.

"You're gonna talk to her today, or do you mean you already did, earlier?"

"Yes," said Katie, still not meeting Mya's eye.

Well, that's clear as mud. "You promise?"

Katie shut the door in Mya's face and she sighed. Of course things wouldn't be that easy. She knew herself that sometimes just asking for help was a huge step just by itself. It was a tough line to walk, trying to encourage Katie but not scare her off, so Mya left it for the time being. *There's a saying about picking your battles, right?* Trying to get both Lynne and Aunt Minnie on side was already a tall order for one day. Mya wasn't honestly sure what to expect from either of them.

Back in her room, Mya got Emma's nappy changed and made sure there were enough supplies in her old school bag to last for the duration. Richard texted just as she got to the main door, to say he was outside, and Mya went over to him, making sure he didn't step foot in the courtyard lest it set Katie off.

"Hey," Rich greeted, cool as a cucumber. It was nice to see—Mya definitely missed him being chill around her, or even just being around her in general—but his calmness had the side effect of always making her feel super tense by comparison. Not that she thought Richard was ever aware of that, and it wasn't exactly something she was gonna tell him. Like, *Hey, change this fundamental part of you that I love so I can be a little more comfortable, please.* Yeah, not gonna happen.

"Hey," said Mya, handing Emma over and ignoring her wayward thoughts. It felt weird—the handover. The longest she'd spent apart from her was when she'd had that awful meeting with her dad at Jane's office, and even then Emma had just been upstairs. *Maybe I* am *tense.*

Richard took a firm grip of the carrier in one hand and shouldered the bag of supplies across his opposite arm. "Is this everything?"

Mya nodded. "You gonna be okay? What's the plan?"

Rich smiled. "My parents want to meet her, of course."

"Of course," said Mya, glad of the fact, even if she was still curious if they'd softened on the possibility of ever seeing Mya herself. *Something to explore another day. Today's battles are already picked,* she reminded herself.

"I'm just gonna take her back to the house," said Rich. "The twins are excited, too. I keep telling them she's not a doll they can play with, but do they listen?"

Mya chuckled. She always loved hearing stories of Richard's sisters, in all their terrible, adorable glory. "I'm sure they'll be fine. You'll take pictures?"

"Duh." Rich stuck his tongue out a little and Mya laughed more, feeling lighter by the moment.

"Okay, well, send me copies or something."

"Sure," said Rich, and he leaned in for a goodbye kiss like they'd shared a thousand times before, only to freeze at the last moment.

Mya could feel the barest whisper of his breath against her lips, and feeling dizzy with the memories it conjured, she tilted her face up to close the final inch separating them. It was a short, simple peck, but much like their first kiss, it was so much more than that, too.

All too soon, they were leaning away again, mouths quirked up at the sides and gazes shyly avoiding each other.

"Well, um...." Richard cleared his throat, no longer looking quite so composed.

Mya took a little pride in the reaction. "Yeah," she said. "I'll, uh, text you when I get back."

"Right."

They stood still for a moment longer, then Mya heard Rich whisper 'fuck it' under his breath and he kissed her again—another goodbye peck, but intentional. Meaningful. Intentionally meaningful!

Mya was grinning to herself as she walked to the hospital. She stopped by the gift shop and looked for the nicest thing she could afford, which turned out to be a tiny bouquet of fake flowers. Mya worried they weren't enough, but then recalled what Lynne had done for Bernice, with her toilet roll banner, and figured she was more of an 'it's the thought that counts' kind of person.

Regardless, Mya paid for the flowers and followed the signs to the maternity unit. Even though it was the same hospital Mya herself had been in, it didn't feel like the same place at all. Mya had been admitted through a different entrance, and had never experienced the place as a visitor. She had to sign in at a little desk, and then sit on the stiffest waiting room chair known to mankind.

After a while, a nurse showed Mya into the ward proper. She passed Adela, who smiled and welcomed her back, asking briefly how Emma was. Mya was surprised that she even remembered them—she figured the staff must see tons of mums come through the doors, and hadn't considered herself all that noteworthy. It warmed her insides.

"Is Doris here?"

Adela shook her head. "Not today, but I can tell her you were asking after her."

"Yeah, do," said Mya, trying to mask her disappointment.

"You're not back in with complications, I hope?"

"Nah." Mya waved a hand. "Visiting a friend. Lynne. Uh, Lynnette Kirk."

"Ah," said Adela with a big smile. "Our troublemaker. Bed three, 'round the corner."

Mya went around the corner and immediately had her attention grabbed by a wealth of cuteness. Her eyes were drawn to the baby in the crib by bed three, and so taken up with watching him—she thought he looked like a boy, though it was always hard to tell when they were so young—Mya didn't pay any attention to Lynne at all for a solid minute.

"Wow," said Mya when she finally looked up. "You look amazing."

"I know," said Lynne, grinning. "Childbirth worked wonders." She gestured to the flowers. "Those for me?"

Mya handed them over. "I'm sorry they're not real."

"I'm not," said Lynne. "Can keep 'em forever, this way."

That made Mya laugh, the weight of apprehension easing off her a little. "I was worried you might not want to see me."

"Why?"

"Well, you know…" Mya wasn't sure she wanted to bring it up again, but Lynne was staring at her, clearly with no idea what she was talking about. "The whole 'I'll never forgive you' thing?"

Lynne hooted with laughter, making some of the other women on the ward glare disapprovingly at her. Lynne didn't seem to see. "Did I say that?" She shook her head. "Wasn't in my right mind, duck. Take no notice."

Mya breathed a sigh of relief. "Seriously, though, you look really great. When I'd just had Emma, I was a mess. This totally isn't fair."

Lynne preened at the compliment and nodded at the crib. "You like him then?"

"He's gorgeous. Can I hold him? What's his name?"

Lynne picked him up and handed him over. "Called him Jackson, after me boyfriend."

Mya blinked, looking up from Jackson to try and determine if Lynne was joking. She was smiling—a lot—but seemed serious enough.

"Boyfriend?" Mya prompted, a sinking feeling in her gut. *She didn't get back together with the abusive asshole, did she? Please, please no.*

"Was near out me head when they brought me in here," said Lynne. "They asked if I wanted anyone, and he was the only one I could think of. The good egg I told you about. Decent sort, you remember?"

"Oh!" *Oh, thank fuck.* "Yes, I remember you mentioning him. Not Jackson's dad, then?"

"Ha!" said Lynne. "Not a chance. Jackson—the older one, I mean—came in, held me hand, and said he'd do whatever I wanted—change nappies, the lot—if I took him back."

"Wow," said Mya. "He must really love you."

Lynne's smile turned wistful. "Don't know why, but he seems to, yeah."

"Oh, you're very lovable," said Mya, meaning it, at which point Lynne looked genuinely choked up. They sat in companionable silence, Mya gently rocking Jackson in her arms while Lynne composed herself.

"But what about you?" she asked after a while. "Who you got minding Emma?"

Mya grinned, delighted that she had her own piece of good news to share. She and Richard might not be officially back to calling each other boyfriend and girlfriend, and she

150

was scared to jump the gun, but things certainly seemed to be heading that way. *So long as Emma behaves and doesn't send him running for the hills.*

"She's with her dad. I saw him before I came here."

Lynne tilted her head.

"What?" asked Mya, self-conscious of being studied.

"You kissed," she said.

"What?" Mya felt her cheeks burn. "How did you–?"

Lynne tapped her nose. "Can't kid a kidder. I can always tell. So, how was it?"

Mya gaped at her friend, shaking her head a little.

"Oh, come on," said Lynne, "I need details. Dish the goss."

"There is no 'goss'," Mya insisted. "It was just a peck. Well, technically two pecks."

"Good start," said Lynne, absolutely delighted with herself. "You'll tell me when there's more?"

Mya laughed. "You're ridiculous. But yes. I'll tell you if–"

"When," Lynne corrected.

"Fine, *when* something else happens."

"Good. Now give him here. I need to get a quick feed in before me boyfriend comes back."

Mya took that as her cue to leave, so happy that Lynne had more than just her as a visitor.

When she got outside, Mya turned her phone on, surprised when it instantly started buzzing in her hand. She was so caught off guard by the phone call, it didn't occur to her until after she'd hit 'accept' that the number was withheld.

In the brief moment between the call connecting and a familiar voice saying "hello," Mya's mind shot off in two directions, one towards Richard's family getting in touch because something was wrong with Emma, and the other option being Kian having stepped up his threatening texts to threatening phone calls, the next evolution in intimidation. Both scenarios spelled doom, and Mya felt her breath catch as she waited to hear which one was about to befall her when the 'hello' broke through her thoughts enough to have her reevaluate things.

"Hello?" Mya said in return.

"Oh, Mya, my girl. It's so good to hear your voice."

Mya was speechless for what felt like an age. It was definitely her mum—the person she wanted to hear from most in the world and the very key to a safe, happy future Mya needed—but she sounded off somehow. It took Mya yet another moment to figure out what about her mum's voice was unsettling her, finally realising that apart from Mya not being used to her mother saying much at all, Akosua had dropped the English accent Kian had forced on her, reverting to her native Ghanaian tone, though maybe a little softer than before. Definitely not as pronounced as Aunt Minnie had sounded. Maybe some kind of hybrid accent?

"Mya, are you there?"

Mya had to sit down on some stone steps and count her breaths to stop them coming out all at once. "Mum?"

"Yes, sweetie, I'm here."

"Mum," Mya repeated, tears appearing in her eyes of their own accord and tracking their way down her cheeks. Mya would normally be embarrassed by such a reaction, especially in public, but couldn't find the will to care just then. "Mum, I can't believe it. It's really you?" Mya had to dig out a tissue from her pocket and wipe her nose. "Where are you? Can I see you?"

"Yes," said Akosua, making Mya's heart leap.

She stood up on shaky legs. "Where? When? Wherever you are, I'll come over now."

Akosua paused, but Mya got the sense she was pondering the answer, not rethinking the plan all together. "That cafe," she said at last. "What's it called? The one I used to take you to, near the cathedral?"

Mya's face split wide open in a grin. "I know exactly which one you mean." They hadn't been there in so long. Years!

"Twenty minutes?" asked Akosua. "Or do you need longer?"

"No." Mya wiped her nose again. "I can be there in twenty." She started walking right away, not wanting to waste a moment.

Mya didn't really want to hang up, in case something happened. She had no idea exactly what kind of tragedy could befall either her or her mother in the space of twenty minutes, and told herself the fear was silly, but it hung around her shoulders nonetheless.

Akosua dialled off and Mya took a few more measured breaths, even as she hurried her steps. All of the things she'd planned to say to Minnie were out, and a thousand new questions were buzzing in her head, leaving Mya not exactly sure where to start, but she continued on her way, confident that as soon as she saw her mother, all the rest would fall into place.

Either that or I'll weep all over her and make such a scene they kick us out.

154

Chapter Eighteen

Mya got to the cafe first, only realising as soon as she sat down that she had no money to actually order anything, the last of her cash having gone on the flowers for Lynne. Mya tried her best to ignore the disapproving look the waitress gave her when she asked for just tap water, hoping that her mum wouldn't be too long and would at least be buying a cup of coffee.

To help pass the time, and give her nervous fingers something to do, Mya turned the menu over in her hands. A couple of flavoured tea variations had been added over the years, but the food on offer was largely the same. Mya's stomach rumbled at the thought of chips and cheese, or a burger. She placed a hand on her belly and looked up, embarrassed, to see if anyone had noticed or cared.

No one so much as batted an eyelid, so Mya's eyes tracked back to the door, where Akosua appeared at last. Mya gasped as she took in the large scar running horizontally across her mother's face. She stood up, feeling the need to do something about it, but not knowing what—the scar was a scar, not an open wound, or a scab. Akosua was long past needing patched up, but logic didn't diminish the instinct any.

Akosua came the rest of the way in and over to where Mya was standing, throwing her arms around her in a hug. A choked sound of surprise escaped Mya at the greeting. It was just so unlike anything her mother would do, or had done, in a long time.

Akosua kept her hands on Mya's shoulders but leaned away after a while, to inspect her. "My girl, look at you." One hand rose to Mya's head.

"I know," said Mya, "my hair is awful."

Charitably, Akosua made no further comment on it. They sat down and Mya breathed a sigh of relief when her mum not only got herself coffee, but offered Mya a drink too.

"You need food? You don't look well. Are you eating right?"

Mya opened her mouth, but the denials on the tip of her tongue were washed away by the sound of her stomach rumbling again.

Akosua tsked and told the waitress to bring a sandwich with "everything in it," not bothering to look at the menu.

Mya felt her cheeks warm. "Mum, you don't have to–"

"Nonsense," said Akosua, waving a hand, "You are my daughter. It's my job to take care of you. Now tell me, what have you been doing with yourself? Where are you staying?"

Far from relieving Mya's qualms about accepting help from her mother, the throwaway line about it being her job to take care of her sparked irritation in Mya's blood, and she decided to turn the questions back on Akosua.

"You first," said Mya. "Tell me where you've been hiding."

Akosua looked a little confused. "You know where."

"Yes," said Mya, her surprise giving the rest of the way over to anger. "I do know, but you never told me. You wouldn't let me see you. All this time and–"

"Please," said Akosua, her tone conciliatory, "you don't understand."

Mya crossed her arms and swallowed back the rest of her rant. "Go on then."

Akosua lifted her teaspoon and moved some sugar cubes around in their little bowl. "I was hoping we wouldn't need to get into it."

Mya blinked at her, speechless, and Akosua sighed.

"I left in a hurry. There was no time to do anything but run."

"Okay," said Mya, because she could imagine that. "But what about after? It's been three weeks, Mum."

Akosua fidgeted with her napkin. "It took a while. To… oh, but how can I explain it? It doesn't matter, Mya. I'm here! We are reunited!"

Mya's heart constricted at the sincerity in her mum's voice and made her own tone gentle in turn. "I know it's hard," she said. "You know I know that. But it matters to me. Please, Mum? I need to understand."

Akosua nodded, pausing to consider her thoughts, and the waitress brought over the drinks to set alongside the cutlery and napkins.

"Your sandwich will be a couple minutes. You allergic to anything?"

Mya shook her head, just wishing the waitress would go away already. Yes, she was hungry, but some things were more important. Mya didn't want to lose this opportunity.

"I went to your aunt," said Akosua, when the waitress did indeed buzz off again. "Mawusi took me in, and I've been there ever since. Has it really been three weeks?"

"Feels like both longer and shorter," said Mya, "but yeah."

"I didn't have any numbers," Akosua went on. "I didn't have time to find an address book."

Well, that made sense. "So you couldn't call me. But why didn't you want to see me when I came to the house?"

Akosua tilted her head to the side in obvious confusion, making the light hit her scar in a new way. Up close it was so much worse.

"The house?" Mya prompted. "Minnie's house. I came to see you and–"

Akosua shook her head. "She didn't tell me."

The rest of Mya's sentence died in her throat and all she could manage for a minute was, "Oh." Then her sandwich came. Mya didn't reach for it right away, but Akosua pushed it in front of her.

"Eat, eat! Please!"

Mya gave in, savouring the first bite. It was actually quite hard to get her mouth around, because they'd taken the 'put everything in it' command to heart. *God only knows how much it's gonna cost, but fuck, I'm so hungry I don't even care.*

Akosua didn't volunteer any information while Mya was eating, so it wasn't until she was done that she could try and find out how her mum *did* finally discover she was looking for her.

"Jane found me," said Akosua, which made Mya choke a little. She took a sip of her drink.

"She did? She gave you my number?"

Akosua nodded. "She said you wanted to talk."

"I did," said Mya. "I do!" *Wow. I can't believe Jane actually came through. Even after the hard time I gave her.*

Akosua smiled, but instead of warming Mya's heart further, it caused a stabbing pain right between her ribs.

"What's wrong?" Akosua asked.

Mya looked down at her side salad and started moving it around her plate with a fork. "It's just been a long time since I saw you smile. I missed it."

Akosua's hand reached out and curled around Mya's, stilling her movements with the fork. Mya looked up and saw tears in her mother's eyes.

"I missed you too, my girl."

Mya had to swallow to stop herself from sobbing. "So," she said after a minute, "how come you didn't go to the police? They wanted to talk to you, too. Once you left, you could have gone to them and we'd have been in touch right away." Mya didn't exactly know that last part was true, but figured it was a pretty good guess, based on what she knew of the system.

Either way, Akosua didn't look convinced. "No," she said, shaking her head. "No police. Too messy."

Mya gaped at her a little. *Too messy?* 'Like your face is messy?' she wanted to say, but resisted. "Mum," she said instead, hoping the single word would somehow convey everything she needed her to know.

"Please, Mya," said Akosua. "I just want to leave it in the past."

"But Mum," Mya pressed. "He's not going to leave us alone. You must know that."

Akosua didn't say anything.

"Mum? Tell me you know."

Akosua turned in her chair to get the waitress's attention, then asked for the bill. "We should go," she said to Mya. "You still haven't told me where you're staying."

"You haven't answered my question," Mya returned. "I'm not moving until you do." It was a total bluff—Mya might not go anywhere, but her mum could walk out any time she liked. Mya just hoped she wouldn't realise that.

Akosua was worrying her napkin again, twisting it between her hands, but she'd gone silent. It wouldn't do. Mya got that Kian was terrifying, but it was all the more reason to try getting him put in jail.

"Did Jane tell you he sent me a text?" Mya asked, trying a different tack, and also trying to do something positive with the desperation growing in her gut.

"A text?"

Mya thought about just telling her about it, but decided to pull out her phone and show it instead. It felt risky, but Mya didn't know how else to emphasise just how hard Kian wasn't going away.

Akosua gasped as she read, causing the waitress to give her a weird look.

"That was after I left," said Mya, suddenly realising they hadn't even come close to talking about how and why she'd left. There was so much ground to cover, and clearly it wasn't going to be achieved in a single sitting. "Listen," Mya went on regardless, "I already said I know it's hard. So I'll stop pushing, okay? Just promise me you'll think about it."

Silence.

"Mum." Mya lowered her voice to a whisper to counteract her sudden desire to scream. "*Please.* I'm just asking you to think."

Akosua hesitated, but eventually nodded.

Mya breathed a deep sigh of relief, honouring her word to let the topic drop there. At least for now. "Have you got a phone? Some way I can contact you?"

"Just Mawusi's home phone," said Akosua. "No mobile."

"Right." That wasn't so good, but Mya tried not to telegraph her disappointment too much.

"You know," said Akosua, "Mawusi wants to protect me. That's probably why she didn't tell me. About you trying to visit."

"I'm not the enemy," Mya snapped, not really meaning to, but damn it stung to be told that. *My aunt thinks my mum needs protection from me? Me!*

160

"I know," said Akosua. "Mawusi.... She doesn't understand."

"Fine," said Mya. Based on her mum's fondness for denial and avoidance, she figured it was pretty safe to assume she hadn't told Minnie anything. And that made it not her fault, technically. Mya didn't want to leave things on a sour note, so struggled for something else to say, finally landing on the pathetic, "Thanks for the sandwich."

Akosua forced a smile. "Growing girl. It's important you eat."

Mya forced a smile right back, not sure how to feel when Akosua didn't try hugging her again when they got outside. *I guess she's not gonna ask me to come stay with her and Minnie, but hey, like Jane says, still some kind of progress.*

It was hard to watch Akosua walk away. Much harder than Mya expected. She wanted so badly to hold her and not let go until A, she felt absolutely safe and secure, or B, she agreed to make a statement in exchange for her freedom. Maybe both.

Yes, it sounded crazy, and of course wouldn't remotely work, but it was another one of those instincts that didn't care about stuff like that.

Mya hadn't asked about her mum's scar, partially because she wasn't sure how to bring it up, and partially because it didn't exactly need explaining. There was no doubt in Mya's mind who had done it and when. It didn't look like it had been looked at in a hospital, which tracked with how difficult it had been to find Akosua after she went to ground. Because if she had shown up in A&E, Mya figured it would have triggered questions being asked. Paperwork, or something. *Probably exactly why she didn't go.*

Mya sighed and pounded the pavement back towards home harder than was strictly necessary. Her mum's attitude was incredibly frustrating, but it wasn't half as aggravating as Mya knowing deep down that she herself hadn't been much better. Her mum was scared and stalling for the exact same reason Mya had waited too long telling Richard about being pregnant. Mya wished she could go back in time and shake herself—talk some sense into her past self—*something!*

Richard was waiting with Emma outside the Mother and Baby Unit by the time Mya got back. The promptness was impressive, seeing as she'd only texted him a couple of minutes before, but also exactly what she needed.

Rich was smiling down at Emma, stroking her hair with the hand he wasn't using to hold her carrier. But then Mya stepped close and he looked up, spell broken. Smile gone.

"You okay?"

"No."

Richard frowned. "What happened?"

"I don't want to talk about it."

He didn't say anything to that, but his expression kind of closed off, and Mya realised her mistake a moment too late. *Of course not talking about stuff's gonna be a sore subject for a while. Forget going to the past and shaking myself, I apparently still need the memo.*

"Sorry," said Mya. "It's just been a hard day. I'm wiped. How's she been?"

Richard's face brightened up again. "Good as gold, so long as you don't count the exploding nappy incident."

Mya laughed. "I hope you're joking, but am so not gonna ask."

"For the best," said Rich.

Mya basked in the feel of broken tension for a moment, then had to come back down to earth. "I should get her inside. Do a feed."

"I gave her one of the bottles you prepared," said Rich.

"Right," said Mya. *Are things awkward again or is it just me?* "Well, I'll need to express more, then. My tits are killing me."

"Sexy," said Rich, tongue in cheek, and Mya laughed again despite herself.

"Oh, you don't know the half of it. Wait until you see my stretch marks!"

Rich's expression changed again, to something with a hint of edge, but not in a bad way. Mya's breath caught at the sudden intensity of his eyes, as she realised somehow the absurd talk of unsexy things had become weirdly heated. *Does this mean he actually wants to see me in my underwear again?*

"I should get back, too," said Rich, after the silence went on too long.

"Right," repeated Mya.

Rich looked unsure if he should try giving her a goodbye kiss, like earlier, and Mya bit her lip, holding his gaze in a way that she hoped would tell him, 'yes, absolutely 100% on board with that plan!'

The message apparently didn't land.

Rich handed Emma over, then passed Mya her bag, his hands going in his pockets and eyes going to his shoes.

Mya told herself not to be too disappointed, but it didn't quite work. *Lynne says there'll be more, and she seems to be magical about knowing stuff. I guess it just needs more time.*

Back in her room, Mya thought over what her mum had said, replaying the conversation and second guessing the whole thing. *What if it really is best to leave things? Pushing Mum to make a statement could put too much strain on her—finally sending her over the edge—and maybe there's no need. Maybe Kian has given up. He sent the text, but that was almost three weeks ago, and there's been nothing since.*

Mya groaned and rubbed her temples, no longer sure what she wanted. Safety, yes, absolutely. But if Kian really had moved on, that meant she was safe from him and just didn't know it. *Guess I'll have to wait and see.*

Ellie Rose McKee

Chapter Nineteen

When the fire alarms went off that night, Mya ignored them as she'd grown accustomed to doing. She still stood by what she'd said to Patsy that first night she'd heard them, about people ignoring them being super dangerous. But after a week, it was honestly easier to set principles aside and stuff a pillow over your head just like everybody else.

Even Emma seemed to have gotten used to them for the most part. They still disturbed her, sure, but not as much, and it was getting easier to settle her again afterwards.

This night, Mya lifted Emma out of her crib and had rocked her halfway back to sleep even with the alarms still blaring when someone in the flat upstairs slammed a door, jolting Emma back to full consciousness.

Mya swore and began pacing. But then another door slammed, and she paused. Was something actually happening? She told herself it was just paranoia—*hoped* it was just that—but she opened her bedroom door and tentatively stuck her head out into the hall just in case.

There it was. The smell of smoke. Faint, but definitely there.

Shit. *Shitshitshit.* Alarm bells went off in Mya's head to match the ones screeching all over the unit. *Okay, think. Could this be something really simple, not an actual emergency? It's not Lynette smoking in her room, because she's still in the hospital, or Bernice burning candles because she's gone. Katie doesn't smoke or have candles, from what I saw, but it could be someone upstairs mucking about.*

Mya wasn't taking any chances at this stage. She gave herself exactly five seconds to stuff her feet in her shoes and lift her phone before making a swift exit down the interior hall, then the entrance hall—where the smell of smoke was definitely stronger—and finally the courtyard.

There were little grey flakes floating down in the courtyard. Ash, Mya realised, after she held out her hand to catch a bit on her palm. Her heart turned cold in her chest and she turned around to see orange-yellow flames licking the side of the building at the far end. At first glance, it looked like they were coming out of the big industrial bin and travelling up the wall from there, but Mya didn't hang around to take a closer look.

She turned to run for the gate and go across the street, well out of range, when she ran—almost headfirst—into Patsy.

"Oh, Mya, thank god." Pasty's eyes were huge and her hair was a crow's nest. She didn't have shoes or a dressing gown on. "Come on!"

Mya hiked Emma higher in her arms and followed. "Is everyone else out?"

Patsy didn't answer, just kept on towards the gate.

A bunch of cars had stopped in the road, and somebody Mya didn't recognise—a man, maybe one of the stopped drivers?—had started trying to turn traffic away from going right past the building, but there was no sign of the police or the fire brigade. Probably because of how many false alarms there had been.

At the assembly point on the other side of the road, the three women who shared the upstairs flat were stood together, two of them leaning on each other and the other one smoking off to the side.

Mya stared at her for a second, then shook her head. She turned back to face the flats, Patsy's face—pale with terror—just to the side of her vision. There wasn't a whole lot to see. From here, there was some of the ash but not as much as was in the courtyard, and the flames weren't visible, though Mya figured that wouldn't be long in changing.

"Have you called 999?" she asked Patsy.

"Yeah. They're coming."

"Right." That was something. Maybe they'd be able to save the building before too much was damaged. And maybe it would make people more careful about setting the alarms off accidentally.

Emma wriggled in Mya's arms, letting her know she was none too happy about having been brought out in the cold in the dead of night. Mya murmured some soothing sounds and looked around again, trying to figure out where Katie was hiding.

"Hey, Patsy?"

"Yeah?"

A niggling, twisting feeling started up in Mya's guts. "Did Katie freak out when she came out? Is someone sitting with her, getting her calm?"

Pasty turned her face away from the building, to look at Mya head-on. Mya gulped, not liking the hollow look in her eyes one bit, but Patsy didn't answer.

"Katie got out, right?" Mya pressed, because of course she couldn't leave it there. She had to know. Katie had to be okay.

Pasty's hands went to her mouth, as if to catch her words, but still none materialised. She was shaking.

"Goddamn it, Patsy! Is she in there or not?"

"Oi!" The woman from the upstairs flat who'd been smoking stepped forward, cigarette now gone. "Don't yell at her."

Mya ignored the woman, but lowered her voice. "Patsy, tell me. Did Katie get out? Have you seen her?"

Pasty shook her head and Mya closed her eyes for a moment.

Right. Her eyes snapped open again, all of her fear and uncertainty pushed aside as she focused on what needed to be done. "You." She pointed at the woman who'd been smoking.

"What?"

"Stay with Patsy. Patsy, can you hold onto Emma for me?" The three women from the upstairs flat looked much more together than Mya's keyworker, but Mya didn't really know any of them. She didn't much like the idea of handing her child to a stranger. Plus, holding Emma might help Patsy stay grounded.

"What are you going to do?" asked smoker-woman.

"I need to get Katie."

The smoker and her flatmates tried to protest, but they were all talking over each other and Mya didn't have time to listen.

"How long until the fire brigade gets here?" Mya asked Patsy. If it was just going to be a minute or two, fine, but Mya couldn't stand around waiting longer than that. Not with Katie and Sarah still inside.

Pasty shook her head again, like she didn't understand the question. *Fuck.* Mya pressed Emma into her hands and ran for the gate to the courtyard before she could change her mind. *Please be okay, please be okay, please!*

In the courtyard, the flakes of ash raining down were bigger and the flames were higher, but they were still far enough away from the door that it didn't seem like a total suicide mission.

Mya took a deep breath, allowed herself a single moment to wonder what the hell she was doing, and then went inside.

She'd only been gone a few minutes—maybe seven, tops—but the corridors were filled with smoke, now. Mya's eyes stung, and she could barely see, but she pushed on, finding her way by memory and running her right hand along the wall. She kept her left hand across her mouth, but it didn't seem to do much good. She was coughing and coughing, dizzy with how much the attack on her lungs was hurting.

Mya hadn't expected it to get to her so fast. The whole place wasn't that big, so she figured she'd be in and out in no time, but the smoke distorted more than Mya's vision, making it hard to think, or figure out how long had passed. She thought she heard fire engines, but honestly wasn't sure if it was just her imagination. The building's own sirens were still going off, after all.

Some distant memory of a school fire safety lecture kicked in, reminding Mya that getting lower to the ground should help, so she dropped and crawled on her hands and knees through the entrance hall and into the ground floor flat. It felt like she was trying to swim through treacle, but finally––*finally!*—she made it to Katie's room. Mya thumped the door but there was no response. She tried the handle, not expecting to find it open, but it was. Mya almost fell through the doorway, then she was stumbling the short distance to Katie's bed and shaking her awake.

Katie was groggy—more so than anyone would be just from pure sleepiness. Mya figured the smoke must have gotten to her; weighed her down, or made her brain fuzzy, because she was acting drunk—slow and uncoordinated—clearly having no idea what was happening.

To Mya's horror, she could feel an increase in temperature from when she'd first come back inside. The fire was getting closer, and she had to get Katie moving now.

Mya took her by the arm, gathered a still-sleeping Sarah under her other arm, and started moving—out of the room and back down the corridor. The colour of the smoke had changed, from a grey-white to almost black, and Mya felt her vision narrow at the edges.

Still, she pushed forward. She figured adrenaline must have hit Katie, because she'd gone from being an almost dead weight to moving with Mya. They and Sarah kept in a tight huddle until they were back in the entrance hall. All three of them were coughing now, hacking and gasping.

Mya tried to ignore the sound, and the pain in her throat and eyes—everything that wasn't moving forward, step by step. Her vision had blanked out completely, and she could feel herself stumbling, but felt in her gut that it was at least in the right direction.

Her arms and legs got heavier and heavier, and Mya wasn't sure at all how long she'd been inside. She was vaguely aware of almost dropping Sarah a couple of times. Mya tried to hold tighter, to both her and Katie, but then something was pulling at them.

Was someone else there? It felt like Mya was in a tug of war, except her heavy arms weren't able to resist much force. In a moment, they were empty, and then it felt like she was floating, or being lifted. Mya had no idea what was happening—if whatever it was was good or bad—but she remembered a bang, and then darkness.

Silence at last.

Chapter Twenty

There were lights, moving and indistinct. And voices. Mya couldn't really tell how many people they belonged to, or what they were saying, she just knew that they hurt her ears. Her eyelids felt like lead, and she tried to turn her head away from the noise, but something was holding her down. A terrified noise escaped her throat all on its own, her breaths came too fast, and Mya tried harder to get her limbs or neck to do something, but then there was a sharp scratch in the crook of her arm, and everything was quiet again.

Dark, but more peaceful than before.

The next time light appeared, it faded in slowly, and didn't seem to be flicking by. It took a moment, but Mya was able to open her eyes and turn her head. She blinked, because everything was kind of blurry, but she could see enough to tell there was a window, and an overhead lamp. A few more blinks and her vision sharpened more, until she recognised the unmistakable privacy curtain of a hospital.

Am I dreaming? How did I get here? When? And... Mya's brain short-circuited, not able to handle any more questions. She heard herself groan, distantly.

Turning onto her side hurt—a lot—but she managed it after a while. Mya tried to sit up, but it was too dizzy-making. Plus, she might not be strapped down anymore, but she was hooked up to things; needles and wires in her arms and across her chest.

The brief thought of her chest jolted something in Mya's brain. She was breastfeeding. How long had it been since she'd done that? And where the hell was Emma? Was she hungry?

One of the monitors off to Mya's right started beeping, and a nurse appeared as if by magic.

"Hi, Mya, my name's Gina. Can you hear me okay?"

Mya tried to answer, but ended up coughing instead. Tears filled her eyes and she didn't know what to do. *What the fuck is happening to me?*

"Just nod or shake your head to answer," said Gina. "Your throat must still hurt after last night."

Last night. Mya thought hard about the words, both separately and together. Last. Night. Last night. Last... *Oh, god!* It came back to her all at once. The fire. There was a fire. And she'd been inside. She'd been with Sarah, and Katie, and––

The monitor beeped again and Gina tsked. "Your heart rate's flying. Try to breathe for me, okay?"

Mya shook her head, both desperate and terrified to know if everyone was okay.

"We need to get your heart rate down," Gina insisted. "If you can't do it, I'll need to give you some help." She produced a needle from her pocket, which only made Mya's panic triple in size, but Gina paused. "Are you going to try breathing for me?"

Mya nodded and Gina counted, helping to time the breaths. After a minute or two, the machine shut up and Gina put the needle away again, unused.

"W-what–?" Mya tried to ask.

"Your social worker is on the way," said Gina. "We called her the second you woke up. She said she'd explain everything."

That didn't sound good, but Mya wasn't in a position to argue.

Gina raised the top half of the bed, so Mya could sit up while still being fully supported, and then Mya closed her eyes to wait. It was insane how tired she felt. Worse than after giving birth and the aftermath of her first counselling appointment combined, which didn't seem possible.

Mya ached to hold Emma, knowing in her gut that it would make anything Jane had to say bearable. Except, what if she was coming to say something bad had happened, and she was gone? Lost, or something. *If she was fine, she'd be beside me, right? We need each other. I'm her only source of food. God, I never should have left her with Patsy.* Mya's head started to spin and she heard the monitor give a warning beep, so she went back to measured breaths.

Despite the terror still washing over her, Mya found herself almost back asleep when Jane walked in. Again, Mya tried to speak but didn't get very far.

"You gave us quite a fright," said Jane, but it was obvious she was trying to keep her tone light. "Do you remember what happened?"

"B-bits," Mya managed. "Is–?"

"Sarah and Katie are fine," said Jane, thankfully cutting to the chase.

Mya felt relief flood through her. "*Emm?*" Mya asked, a little breathlessly, not quite able to form the 'a.'

"Emma is with Richard."

Oh, thank fuck. Mya lay her head back, closed her eyes, and wept.

Jane gave her time to work it most of the way out of her system, then said, "I'm sure you have other questions, but they can wait. The important thing is that you're safe. The doctors seem to think you'll have a full recovery."

Recovery from what, Mya wasn't quite sure. What had the fire done to her? There was the pain, and tiredness, and confusion, but beyond that...

"I'm going to sit right here and catch up on paperwork," said Jane, indicating a chair off to the side, opposite the monitors. "You sleep a little more, see if you can get your throat working, and we'll talk properly."

Mya stared at her, trying hard to communicate telepathically, and it seemed to work because Jane said, "Emma really is fine. The doctors checked her over and gave a full bill of health. No ill effects from the smoke."

All of the tension in Mya's back and shoulders eased and she sagged, slipping a little way down the bed where sleep caught her.

Later—she had no idea how long, an hour or a day—Mya opened her eyes feeling much less like she'd been run over by a truck. The seat next to her was empty, so Mya tried calling out. It was raspy, but she managed a "Hello?"

Jane appeared from behind the curtain. "Hello. I was just checking in with your nurses."

"How...?"

"Still fine," said Jane. "All your vitals are normal. They said not to be worried about you sleeping so much. Apparently that's normal, too."

"What...?"

"What happened?"

Mya nodded.

"Well," said Jane, sitting back down in her visitor's chair, "Katie hasn't been able to tell us anything much, but from what the firemen were able to figure out, you'd gotten her and Sarah almost to the door when smoke started to overwhelm you. Two firemen entered the building and lifted you the rest of the way out—just seconds before the fire reached the gas supply. If it had been any longer…" Jane didn't finish the thought, but the unsaid words lay heavy between them.

It didn't really feel real. Mya could remember more of it now, but it felt like visualising a story someone had told her rather than an event she'd been there for herself.

"You're quite the hero," said Jane, her voice turning light again. "The local paper want to put you on the front page."

Mya coughed on the air in her mouth and sat forward, her eyes feeling wild in her head.

"Now, calm down," said Jane, before Mya could say anything. "You don't need to worry about being found."

Mya blinked. Just what the hell did that mean? That Kian wasn't looking for her anymore? How would they know that?

"They've arrested him," said Jane, doing the telepathic thing again.

It took Mya a minute to process what she was saying——and the bits she was leaving out. Kian had been arrested. For the text? That didn't seem right. Why now when they hadn't before? There must have been new evidence, or something must have happened. What happened? Wait. Is she saying he was involved with the fire?

"When your mum heard about what happened, she made a statement to the police," Jane explained. "They went to search Kian's house and found not only evidence that he started the blaze, but proof that he sent you the threatening text."

Holy shit! Mya's heart thumped hard in her chest, suddenly feeling too big for such a small space. She felt easily a dozen things at once—anger, relief, disbelief, joy, and amazement being the ones she could identify.

Jane sat in silence for a while as the revelation settled down somewhere in Mya's brain, so she could start to maybe think again.

"I realise it's a lot to process," Jane continued at last. "I debated leaving things here for today, but there are some people who'd very much like to see you, and I think you'd be better off seeing them, too.

"Huh?"

"One minute," said Jane, and she slipped out again.

Mya waited, eventually hearing the door open, then Richard appeared from behind the curtain, Emma in his arms.

Mya almost passed out with the fresh wave of emotion that hit her. Yes, she'd believed Jane when she said Emma was safe, but it was a different thing to actually see her. And Richard with her! It was almost more than Mya could handle.

The smile on Rich's face when he came in dimmed as he looked at her. "Mya?"

She shook her head. "Fine." She coughed. "I-I'm fine."

Richard sat down and took Mya's hand with his free one. "Never do anything like that again, okay?"

Mya nodded, tears tracking down her cheeks. Fuck, she loved him. Him and Emma and them all being together. If she could just keep this moment, she vowed to never do another stupid thing in the rest of her whole stupid life.

"Hey," Rich whispered, leaning close to press his forehead to hers. "It's okay. You're okay." He kept repeating it, until at some point it started to sound true.

Mya let go of Rich's hand and indicated the small space beside her in the bed. It took some manoeuvring, but he perched beside her, Emma cradled between them, and they basked for a while not saying anything at all.

"Listen," Rich said at last. "My mum and dad were talking. Your place is totalled, but they wouldn't want you going back there anyway."

Mya tilted her head at him, trying to find meaning by searching his eyes from a different angle. "Wouldn't?" she questioned.

"Mya," said Rich, taking her hand again. "We want you to move in with us. You and Emma both. To be close, you know? The place is small, but we can make it work."

A lump formed in Mya's throat, removing her ability to even use the broken words she'd been managing, but she nodded, delighted to see Richard's eyes light up in response.

"They, um—my folks—they said they didn't want us sharing a bed, but there aren't a whole lot of options. I've agreed to sleep on the sofa, but think it'll be about a week before my dad wants his living room back and they'll ease up on us having a room to ourselves."

Something like a surprised laugh bubbled its way up and Mya grinned. It seemed an utterly ridiculous thing to focus on, but it didn't matter. Three weeks ago, she could barely imagine a future where she got to keep Richard in her life at all, but now they were fine-tuning the logistics of being under the same roof.

Rich looked unsure. A little shy. "You really don't mind?"

Mya leaned forward and pressed her lips to his, not caring that they were dry and her face was probably a state from crying.

Richard didn't seem to mind either. He kissed Mya back, closed-mouth, until Emma started squirming between them and they pulled away to look at her.

God, she was perfect. Mya held out her finger for Emma to grasp and it was like her chest reset to the right size, where everything fit and no vital organs were in danger of being crushed.

"Mya," said Rich softly and she looked up at him again.

"Yeah?" Mya whispered.

He brought her hand to his lips and kissed her palm. "I love you. I'm sorry I was an idiot before. Not giving you a chance to explain, or–"

Mya gently slipped her hand free and pressed her fingers to his lips. "'S'okay."

"You promise?" asked Rich, and she nodded, smiling.

Mya nodded and kissed him again. Despite everything, it really was okay. Better, even! Mya didn't have much of a plan beyond getting discharged into the care of Richard's parents, but screw plans, Mya had solid hope to hang onto. And that sense of safety she'd been chasing. For once, it really felt like things might work out—for Mya and Emma and Richard, probably her mum, too, and everyone else she'd met along the way. The thought was intoxicating and Mya had to pull back from the kiss to catch her breath.

This was it. Her hell was over, and she'd survived.

Epilogue

It was slow going, but a week and a half after being rushed to hospital, and seven days after she'd been released, Mya climbed the stairs to her counsellor's office and took a seat.

Mitch's secretary immediately materialised with both juice and tea aplenty. "If you need anything else, let me know. Mitch will be right with you."

"Thanks," said Mya, lifting the juice to loosen up her vocal cords. Her throat was a lot better now—almost back to normal after all of the smoke—but Mya liked to help it along where she could. Both the hot and the cold drink would feel good, though in different ways.

What was harder to get used to was people being extra nice and going out of their way to help. Also not having to bring Emma everywhere. That part was pretty funny, actually, because Mya had mistakenly thought she'd been keeping Emma permanently at her side for her daughter's benefit—

which was true in the practical sense, because of the breastfeeding—but Emma turned out to be perfectly fine staying with Richard's family, and Mya was the one feeling lost not lugging around a baby carrier and old school bag all of the time.

"You look miles away."

Mya looked up to see Mitch had appeared just as suddenly and seemingly from nowhere as his secretary had done.

"I guess I am a little spaced," she admitted. "Side effect of the painkillers."

"Ah, yes," said Mitch, taking his seat opposite, "The accident."

"It wasn't an accident," Mya was quick to correct him, to which Mitch raised his eyebrows. "Fire was started deliberately. Kian's been charged and denied bail. Just yesterday, actually."

"Well," said Mitch, "I stand corrected. How do you feel about it?"

Mya took a moment to give the question due consideration, not automatically settling for the typical 'fine' response. Though, "I think I actually am fine. Genuinely," she said at last.

"I'm glad," said Mitch, smiling. "I've had clients do some pretty crazy things to get out of our sessions, but I've never had anyone rescue people from a fire and almost get blown just up to skip a meeting before."

Mya laughed, feeling weirdly okay with talking about serious things in such an offhand way, but the laughter became a cough and she had to reach for more juice. Mitch was watching her face intently when she looked up from the glass, and she had to assure him again that she was okay. "Really."

"All right," he said. "There are a few directions I can lead today's chat in, but is there anything in particular you want to address first?"

"Not the fire," said Mya, maybe too quickly. "I'm fine to acknowledge it happened, and I'll go into it at some point, probably, but not now. I… is that okay?"

"Of course," said Mitch. "You probably need a bit of distance from it."

"Yeah," said Mya, easing a little further back into her chair. "That."

"Do you mind if I ask about your flatmate?" Mitch questioned, flicking through his notes. "Katie, is it?"

"Yeah," said Mya. "It's fine. She and Sarah are safe, and Katie's getting some treatment for her anxiety. I think it might be more than just anxiety, but I don't know what. She still clams up a lot, but I've seen her since the fire and she seemed better. I think she's almost glad she was forced out of her room, but…" Mya shrugged. "That sounds stupid."

"Not really," said Mitch. "If she was finding being there hard, it follows that being somewhere else might be easier, especially if she's getting help."

"I guess."

"Have you seen your mum again?" asked Mitch. "I know you said when we spoke briefly on the phone that you were worried about her. That was before Jane told me what happened."

"Sorry, yeah. Sometimes I forget who knows what. Mum's okay, I think. Freaked, definitely—she was too upset to visit me in hospital—but my aunt's taking care of her and we've arranged to meet up next week."

"That's great," said Mitch. "Really great. Any other plans?"

"I want to see Lynne again," said Mya. "She's out of the maternity ward and living with her boyfriend. And I want to make more of an effort with Zhara."

Mitch was grinning.

"What?" said Mya, feeling a little embarrassed all of a sudden.

"I'm just impressed. For someone who once told me they had no real support network to speak of, you seem to be doing pretty well for yourself."

"Yeah," said Mya, pausing to think about it. "Yeah, I think I am."

Mitch made another note and looked up again, as if waiting for something else. Mya wasn't exactly sure what—she was pretty sure she'd covered everything in what they'd just said—but she found herself wanting to please her counsellor, pathetic as that might sound.

"I, um… I'm thinking of going back to school."

Mitch's pen paused on his notes, seemingly mid-word. "Really?"

"Maybe," said Mya, backpedaling a little. *Why did I say that?* "I'm thinking about it, anyway."

"Well, you know you'll have as much or as little support from Jane as you need."

"I know," said Mya. "She's been pretty great." *Maybe I can get her a card or something. 'Thanks for not giving up on me, even when I bit your head off,' kind of thing. Hallmark had to have something. They had a card for seemingly every other eventuality.*

Mitch laughed and Mya blinked, looking over at him. "Did I say that out loud?"

"No. Just whatever you were thinking took you very far away again. It looks like you might need some more bed rest."

"Oh." Mya blushed and looked at the clock. "But I still have most of a session left."

"It can wait," Mitch assured her. "Things are good at the minute, and I'm glad, but there's still a lot we've got to talk about. It'll all come in time."

"Yeah," said Mya, feeling exhaustion really hit her just at the thought of it.

"Home and rest," said Mitch, smiling again. "Tomorrow's a new day."

Mya smiled back, despite her tiredness. "One step at a time, right?"

"That's right."

Mya took the sentiment to heart, slowly easing her way out of the room and back down the stairs. *Home and rest,* she thought to herself. *Sounds fantastic.*

The Family Ties Trilogy
will continue in
Book Two: Life Lessons

Subscribe to the author's newsletter for updates at
www.ellierosemckee.com/newsletter

Acknowledgments

I first started this book on the 22nd of May 2016. By the time it finally goes into print (30th March 2021), it will be just under two months shy of being five years old, from first word to publication. So much has happened in that time, and so many people have helped that I'm both thrilled and terrified that now, at this very last hurdle, I'm going to forget to thank someone. Just in case, I ask forgiveness in advance if you feel your name should be below, but you find it missing.* Please know this was not intentional. There's a saying about it taking a village to raise a child, and I feel like it's taken an entire online community to bring forth this book.

But enough preamble. Let me first start with my editor, the wonderful and ever patient Bridget Wilde. I know it's cliché, but I honestly could not have gotten this book into print without her. This book is very literally a different book than the one I handed to her, but it's so much better for all the rewrites. Be, honestly, thank you so much!

Next, I must thank Be's partner in crime, Anna Sheehan, who not only beta-read considerable parts of this book (and a few of its previous iterations), but contributed a large portion of the IndieGoGo funding, *and* provided the lovely quote for the cover as well. I don't know what I've done to deserve you, but if I ever find out, I'll let you know!

I have spent countless nights being encouraged by both Bridget and Anna—often both at the same time— throughout this long process. Thank you both for listening to all my 5am meltdowns.

Going back over ten years to my university days, I want to thank my original critique partner, Mickey Luke Mitchell. I also want to apologise for the things I made you read back then, when I was very much still finding my feet.

Similarly, the dear Liz Griffin who read a lot of my old work, before I quite got the grip on grammar and punctuation I have now. Thank you, and sorry for all the typos I brought into your life.

Speaking of typos, my good friend Jodie Eve, in her innocence, used to get me to beta-read her work. Many, many hours were spent moving around commas that I'm still not quite sure are entirely right, but you believed I knew what I was doing and for that I am so grateful.

I'm proud to have also been buoyed by support from the Arts Council of Northern Ireland, Belfast Writers' Group, Women Aloud NI, SCBWI (both British Isles and Irish chapters), countless Elysian Fields members (you know who you are!), my lone Patreon patron Seanín Hughes, beta readers Tina 'Mini' Scott and Vee Caswell (who both also contributed to my crowdfunding campaign), critique partner Lesley Walsh, life partner and perpetual lemon toasty of the month (don't ask!) my wonderful husband Steve Herron, and writing mentors Felicity McCall and Jo Zebedee.

My darling Stephanie Hibbert did an excellent sensitivity read of this novel for me (i.e. answered all of my ignorant white people questions), and I got expert advice from Cathy Carson, Alicia Rana, and Dr Joanne Holland DVM MD about safeguarding, nursing, social work protocols, and midwifery respectively. Any errors that may have slipped in regarding any of these topics are my own doing, not theirs.

Shout out to Wendy L. Bonifazi RN CLS APR, who kindly proofread this novel for me, and of course the rest of my awesome IndieGoGo Backers: Debi Lamm, Cat Pothier, Liz Weir, Byddi Lee, Shirley-Anne McMillan, Beth Armstrong, Karen Mooney, Mark Davidson, Ryan Miller, Marianne Simpson, Cathy Reilly, Kay Adlington, Elizabeth McGeown, Emma King, Lynda Collins, Anthony Calamis, Wilma Kenny, Kelly Creighton, and my cousin (and fellow author) Kim Graham.

The puddle/ocean advice that Lynne gives Mya in chapter five, I picked up from Tumblr many years ago and have never forgotten, though sadly I haven't the faintest idea who shared it originally—told you I'd forget someone!

Just thank you, thank you, *thank you* all so very much!

*Edited to Add During Second Printing:
Turns out that I did indeed leave at least one person off the list. I have to give a big shout out to my excellent superhero web developer Will 'Power' Hall. And Emma King deserves more thanks as she helped me format the cover files for this book. You're both stars!

Trigger Warnings

- Abuse (Sexual) – Mention of, but no graphic description.
- Adult Language (Swearing) – Mild to moderate in severity. Somewhat infrequent use.
- Child Abuse – Mentions of, but no graphic description.
- Domestic Violence – Mentions of, but no graphic description.
- Medical Trauma and Treatment – Somewhat graphic descriptions, but not gratuitous.

If you have been upset by any of the depictions of the above content, or any other issues raised, please remember that it is okay to reach out and talk to people about it. Whatever country you are in likely has some kind of dedicated support service, which is only a Google search away. Please do not suffer in silence.

www.ingramcontent.com/pod-product-compliance
Lightning Source LLC
Chambersburg PA
CBHW050137110726
47898CB00008B/2570